"ISN'T THIS ALMOST FUN?"

"It's the most *almost* fun I've had all day." He grinned. He suddenly had an overwhelming urge to kiss her. . . . Both sensed danger at the same moment and, as if on cue, spun around, then froze. A dark form that hadn't been there a moment before now moved among the moonshadows.

Nicky wanted to run, but his feet wouldn't obey. Marta let the wood fall from her arms, grabbed both of his hands, and jerked him down. Sliding her arm around his neck, she pulled his cheek next to hers so she could whisper into his ear. "Stay calm and still and it *should* leave us alone." Nicky remained frozen in this awkward position, his arms grasping Marta, her knees clenched between his. *What a way to die* was all he could think.

Other Avon Flare Books by
Dian Curtis Regan

I'VE GOT YOUR NUMBER
THE PERFECT AGE

GAME OF SURVIVAL

DIAN CURTIS REGAN

AN AVON  FLARE BOOK

AVON BOOKS
A division of
The Hearst Corporation
105 Madison Avenue
New York, New York 10016

Copyright © 1989 by Dian Curtis Regan
Published by arrangement with the author
Library of Congress Catalog Card Number: 88-91385
ISBN: 0-380-75585-8
RL: 6.1

First Avon Flare Printing: June 1989

For my parents
Don and Katherine Curtis
with love and thanks

Special acknowledgment to the
Denver WC Club:

Marilyn Butcher, Carolyn Adamo,
Auline Bates, Lalette Hammett Douglas,
Jan Gindorf, the Walrus,
and even Mark Shaw

Chapter 1

Nicky Brooks tightened his grasp on the heavy duffel bag full of softball equipment to keep it from knocking into his hip as he galloped down the steep slope from the Mitchell High School gym to the buses waiting below. In a few minutes, the buses, filled with members of Mitchell's Athletic Club, would be taking off on their annual fall Weekender at Camp Chautauqua in the Colorado Rockies.

Nicky slid the heavy duffel bag into the opened belly of the bus, feeling privileged at being asked to supervise the loading of supplies, since he was only a sophomore. Shaking out his strained arm muscles, he wished his supervisor status had gotten him out of some of the hard work.

"Hey, Nick!"

Turning at the sound of his name, Nicky leaned against the bus and folded his arms against the brisk October wind. He watched his best friend, Luker Ames, run down the slope hand-in-hand with Erin Leigh.

Framing the two, aglow in the light of the late afternoon sun, he snapped a mental picture—a habit he'd developed whenever he was without his camera and an interesting scene attracted him.

Nicky zoomed in on the couple as they came closer.

1

He was always struck with the similarity in their looks—same brown eyes and hair. He thought they looked more like brother and sister than boyfriend and girlfriend.

Feeling a twinge of envy at the sight of Luker and Erin so happy together, Nicky reminded himself for the umpteenth time that this was the weekend he planned to break the ice with Shana Adams, something he'd been dying to do ever since the blond-haired goddess had transferred to Mitchell High last spring. The Weekender offered a perfect opportunity to monopolize her attention.

Laughing at a private joke, Erin and Luker came to an abrupt stop at the foot of the hill, almost running into him.

Erin smiled, trying to catch her breath as she reached to ruffle Nicky's dark, close-cropped hair. She always teased him about keeping it short for track.

Nicky caught her slender wrists together in one of his hands, then ruffled her short hair in return. She squirmed away, giggling, until she broke his grasp.

He liked Erin. He could talk to her as a friend without feeling self-conscious because she was a member of the opposite sex—not like Shana, who could melt his socks just by walking by.

Nicky stopped his teasing when he realized Erin and Luker were empty-handed. "Hey, why am I doing all the work?"

"That's the end of the supplies." Luker grinned at him as he pointed toward a few students heading their way, arms full of boxes. "It's time to load bodies now. Come on." He took Erin's hand again. "It's freezing out here. Let's grab some good seats."

They seemed to forget Nicky as they hurried toward the front of the sophomore–junior bus. Nicky'd gotten

2

used to being ignored by Luker ever since Erin had come into his friend's life. He knew Luker wasn't being mean; he was just infatuated. Nicky wanted to care about someone as much as his friend cared about Erin. His heart sped up as the image of Shana flickered across his memory. She was a pretty nice candidate for his affection.

"Hey!" He hollered after his friend. "Save me *two* seats, remember?" Luker knew about Nicky's plan to spend the Weekender with Shana. He gave Nicky a thumbs-up sign before disappearing into the bus.

Scanning the wave of noisy students jostling down the hill, Nicky hoped for a glimpse of Shana's shimmering hair in the crowd. He was anxious to board the bus, just in case Luker, who obviously had other things on his mind, forgot to save the seats. But since Mr. German, the Athletic Club counselor, had asked Nicky to supervise the bus loading, he had to wait until all supplies were on.

"Out of the way!"

Nicky jumped at the command as three scrawny freshmen, huffing and puffing, dumped boxes of food at his feet. As he opened his mouth to question why lowly freshmen were loading the buses, his eye caught the person who'd yelled the command—Scruggs. Nicky watched the giant brute saunter down the slope, his overdeveloped muscles making his body appear two sizes larger than his head. He growled instructions at his chosen subordinates like a drill sergeant. Leave it to Scruggs to strong-arm a bunch of freshmen into doing his work for him and to make them think he's in charge.

Scruggs liked to play the role of the popular jock. Unfortunately, he wasn't very good at any sport he tried. His size, plus his ability to tackle and crush

3

opposing players, had gotten him onto the football team, but he seemed to vent his frustration at not being a star by harassing others.

Nicky ignored Scruggs' rude comments and rescued a bulky box of oranges from a thankful-looking freshman girl. As he bent his lanky form to slide the box into the bus, Scruggs tackled him from the side, knocking him to the ground, scattering oranges across the yellowing grass like colorful croquet balls.

Nicky rolled once, then rose to his knees in anticipation of another strike. Every cell in his body filled with an intense dislike for Scruggs, who'd been pulling the same kind of tricks on him for as long as he could remember.

Scruggs merely laughed, making Nicky feel stupid kneeling on the grass. "Well, Nicholas, aren't we clumsy today?" he quipped, gesturing at the oranges.

Nicky felt his face flush as he came to his feet, sizing up his opponent. He had a strong urge to scatter pieces of Scruggs across the grass like the oranges.

The unspoken competition between the two had begun in the seventh grade, after Nicky's family moved to Colorado from Texas. Nicky, with his light frame, was the fastest runner and the highest jumper, immediately attracting attention and praise from the P.E. teachers.

Scruggs' competitive mind had made him want to win, but his pre-teen body had been more fat than muscle. He intimidated most of the other guys until they let him win, but the idea of faking a loss insulted Nicky's sense of honor. Besides, it didn't matter to Nicky if he were running around a track, down a football field, or around the bases; once he started, nothing could stop him. All his senses became tuned

4

to the challenge of taking longer and longer strides, feeling his heartbeat, his breath, and his footfalls lock together in rhythm. Nicky couldn't pretend to lose for anyone, much less a chubby jerk who frightened all the other guys. How could Nicky have known he was antagonizing someone who would later turn into a human Mack truck—thanks to a growth spurt and weight lifting?

Over the top of Scruggs' head, Nicky saw Mr. German and Ms. Egan, the girls' counselor, trotting down the hill. Not wanting to get into trouble for fighting, or risk getting left behind, Nicky turned away from Scruggs and collected the scattered oranges. "Why don't you grow up?" was all he said. He tried to make his voice sound deeper than it was.

Scruggs reached to knock on the bus window above him, getting the attention of two girls. "Hey, Nicholas, if you play your cards right, this may be the best weekend you've ever had."

"Don't ruin the Weekender for the rest of us." Nicky shot Scruggs a disgusted look. "If you're caught with beer—or anything else—it's a one-way ticket home. You know the rules."

Scruggs backed toward the bus door, kicking a stray orange further away. "Who needs that," he yelled, "when we're gonna have *girls?*"

Chapter 2

Mr. German lumbered down the slope. His armor-like layers of bulky clothing made him resemble an overfed armadillo. Next to him came Ms. Egan, looking more like a student than a teacher. Her blond hair was caught up in a banana comb, and she wore faded blue jeans and Keds. Ms. Egan gave Nicky a quick wave before boarding the senior bus. Mr. German stopped next to him. "Here." He thrust a clipboard toward Nicky, then leaned down to inventory the already inventoried boxes. Nicky took the opportunity to fan through the permission slips attached to the clipboard until he found the one he was looking for:

We give our permission for Shana Adams to attend the Weekender at Camp Chautauqua.

An unreadable signature was scrawled across the bottom. Nicky touched his fingers to Shana's name, caressing the scribbled letters as he counted them, playing a game he'd learned in elementary school. If a girl's name had the same number of letters as a guy's name, she was destined to be his forever girlfriend. Nicky and Shana. Five and five. It worked.

Suddenly remembering where he was, Nicky jerked

his hand away. He glanced around to see if anyone was watching, feeling foolish for playing such a childish game.

As Mr. German finished counting boxes stored on both buses, Nicky flipped through the remaining permission slips. An unfamiliar name caught his attention. "Martinella Lee Prigmore," he read aloud, pulling the slip from the stack. "Hey, Mr. G, who's this with the weird name?"

"Huh?" Mr. German straightened, looking flushed underneath his layers of armor. He tilted his head, holding the slip at arm's length to read it through bifocals perched precariously on the tip of his nose. "Oh, the Prigmore girl. She moved here from New Jersey a few days ago, and more than qualifies for the Athletic Club. She's quite talented in sports, I hear. Swimming is her specialty." He retrieved the clipboard from Nicky, refastening the permission slips.

"Let's go!" Ms. Egan leaned out the first window of the senior bus and pointed to her watch. Nicky slammed the cargo doors, then followed Mr. German as he boarded the sophomore/junior bus. Sidestepping down the aisle, dodging arms and legs, Nicky spotted two empty seats across from Erin and Luker. "Thanks," he whispered as he slipped into the first seat, feeling guilty that he'd doubted his friend's memory.

Now, where was Shana? He wished everyone would quit moving around so he could spot her. Was she late? Perfect. The only seat left was the one next to his.

Mr. German shushed the students and called roll. Everyone laughed when he said "Sidney Scruggman" because no one but a teacher would dare call Scruggs his real name to his face. Scruggs threw back a few threats, but was careful to keep his voice low. If Mr.

German had heard, he probably would have kicked Scruggs off the bus, making it a much more pleasant trip as far as Nicky was concerned.

As the driver started the engine, Nicky realized Shana's name hadn't been called. He stepped into the aisle so he could see over everyone's head, but still couldn't find her. Had she boarded the senior bus by mistake? Erin leaned over Luker to whisper to him. "I heard Shana had to stay home tonight because her family is having company. Her dad's driving her to Chautauqua in the morning."

Nicky's high hopes of sharing the trip with the girl of his dreams instantly plummeted. Falling back, he sprawled across both seats, remembering that those who weren't paired off with someone by late Friday night spent the whole Weekender feeling left out. It was like showing up at the prom as the only person without a date while everyone stared at you all night, cracking jokes behind your back.

The reason he could recall this unwritten Weekender tradition so well was because that's exactly what had happened to him last year. Luker had paired off with Kelli Tafoya, which had made Nicky feel even more left out because Kelli hadn't spoken to him since he'd accidentally set her pet hamster free during a backyard birthday party in the eighth grade.

"Excuse me." A sudden squeaky voice pierced his gloomy daydream.

Startled, Nicky looked up into a freckled face, surrounded by a frizzy cloud of reddish-blond hair. The girl wore lavender-framed glasses and had a mouthful of braces and an armful of books and jackets.

"This is the only seat left." She teetered as the bus lurched, almost dropping everything into his lap. "Please move over?"

Nicky bolted upright as quickly as if an alarm had gone off, then slid into the window seat while this unannounced stranger sat next to him, smiling.

He stared at her, shocked at the prospect of sharing his seat with a girl other than Shana. Nicky had previewed the bus ride in his mind a million times, rehearsing all the charming, clever things he was going to say, never once imagining the events would not happen the way he'd planned.

He felt annoyed, even though the girl was kind of cute. Feeling disloyal to Shana for even noticing another girl, Nicky pretended a sudden interest in the passing scenery, wanting to be left alone.

"Hi," the girl began, obviously not able to read his leave-me-alone thoughts. "My name is Martinella Lee Prigmore. What's yours?"

The name caught Nicky's attention. "*You're* Martinella Lee Prigmore?"

"Oh!" She looked surprised. "You mean you've heard of me?"

"No. Yes. I mean I . . . uh . . . I heard your name somewhere. It's kind of unusual." He couldn't think of any other way to explain it, but he wanted to put a quick end to this polite small talk and return to his private musings.

"I know; I hate my name," she continued anyway. "It's been handed down for generations. Should have died a long time ago. My friends back in New Jersey call me Marta."

"Good. I'll call you Marta." Nicky's tone was short. Why was he feeling such animosity toward this girl? She didn't deserve it.

"Does that mean we're friends?" She held out a freckled hand.

"No, it doesn't." He leaned away, hugging the

9

window, and frowned back at her, hoping she'd get the hint. "Look, will you please stop talking?" Subtle hint, he groaned to himself.

Nicky concentrated on the dark buildings which seemed to be flying past the window. What was wrong with him? How could he be so nasty to a stranger? Any other time he would have enjoyed talking to her and getting to know someone new. But right now he wanted to feel sorry for himself in private. Why couldn't she see that? And why couldn't she be Shana?

The silence between them seemed loud. Feeling guilty, Nicky dared a glance in her direction. She was staring at her hiking boots. "Look," he said softly. Out of the corner of his eye he could see Luker leaning forward, raising his eyebrows up and down, winking, and nodding his head toward Marta. He hoped Marta hadn't noticed what his weird friend was doing.

He swallowed a laugh directed at Luker. "I didn't mean to be unfriendly. I know you're new here and it wasn't very brilliant of me to be rude." The failing light did not allow him to see her face clearly. "I apologize."

She didn't answer.

"Can we start over? My name is Nicky Brooks. I . . . yes, we can be friends. Marta's a nice name, really." He touched her arm gently so she would know he really meant it.

"It's okay." She half-smiled. Lights from a passing car reflected off her glasses.

Nicky felt pleased he'd smoothed things over. "I'm going to sleep now," he said, hoping it would be a good way to avoid further conversation. He slipped off his jacket, arranging it over his shoulders like a blanket. The constant rumble-swaying of the bus calmed his annoyance. He took a deep breath, letting

10

his thoughts pull him back inside his head. The Weekender he'd been counting the days for was certainly getting off to a less than spectacular start.

Nicky tried to sleep, but Scruggs and his rowdy friends had taken over the back of the bus, making sleep impossible. The group was trying to be as obnoxious as they could—and was succeeding.

Marta was reading a book in the circle of dim light from the small lamp above her seat. Scruggs kept yelling at her to turn it off so it would be darker in the back of the bus. But from what Nicky could see and hear, they weren't having much luck with any of the girls back there. All bark and no bite, he thought.

Giving up on sleep, he stretched as best he could in the cramped seat, watching Marta from the corner of his eye. "What are you reading?" he asked, his curiosity getting the better of him.

"Tips on Backpacking and How to Survive." She flipped the book shut to show him the cover illustration of a young couple decked out in matching backpacks hiking in a sunlit forest. "It's smart to be informed when you're spending time in the mountains."

Nicky chuckled. "They're not going to dump us in the middle of nowhere. We'll be staying in cabins, so I don't think we'll be worrying about how to survive." He laughed again at her naivete. Typical Easterner concept about life in the rugged Rocky Mountains, he thought, even though he, himself, was from mountainless West Texas. "The cabins are pretty sparse, but we'll have almost all the comforts of home. Don't worry about it."

She pulled off her glasses to clean them. Under the bright reading light, her eyes were a maple syrup brown, the same shade as her freckles. "But," she

11

argued, "we'll be doing a lot of hiking and exploring. Especially on the scavenger hunt."

"Hey, Nicholas!" Scruggs yelled, interrupting them. "Tell your girlfriend to turn off the light. Or are you afraid you won't know what to do with the lights out?"

A sudden burst of laughter from everyone on the bus made Nicky jerk away from Marta. He *hated* being laughed at. And he hated Scruggs for calling him Nicholas—a habit he'd picked up from a middle school teacher who believed in calling all her students by their full names. She'd called Scruggs, Sidney, but none of the kids in the class dared follow suit after two boys and a girl went home with bloody noses.

"Who's your new girlfriend, Nicholas?" Scruggs continued in his jeering voice. "Little Red Riding Hood?"

Nicky slouched in his seat, hoping Marta would get the hint and turn out the light, even though under different circumstances, he would have fought for her right to leave the light on as long as she pleased. Awareness that he was sharing his seat in the limelight with a stranger and not with Shana returned to stab at his heart.

The light clicked off as Marta whispered a faint, "I'm sorry."

Chapter 3

The buses finally groaned their way up the last dark hill to Camp Chautauqua. Nestled in a steep canyon in the Rocky Mountains, the rustic camp was over a hundred years old. Last year, on his first Weekender, Nicky learned that Chautauqua had been built as a rest station for stagecoach passengers on their way to the mining camps during the gold rush to the Rockies in the 1860s. The camp had been modernized twenty years ago and named Chautauqua, an Indian word meaning "a place where people gather together for learning."

The dim moonlight lit the campsite as the buses chugged to a halt. The main lodge, built of giant logs, overlooked a grassy meadow bordered by a rock-filled stream. Last year, on a lark, he and Luker—minus Kelli Tafoya—panned the stream for gold nuggets and had been ecstatic when they'd actually found several tiny pieces of gold ore.

Behind the lodge, back in the forest, were quaint cabins heated by wood stoves. Nicky looked forward to rolling out his sleeping bag onto one of the bunk beds. It made him feel as if he were roughing it, but after five minutes he knew he'd be wishing for his comfortable bed back home.

Hopping off the bus, he battled for a turn to pull his

belongings from the side compartment. Then he searched for Luker, eager to share memories of last year with him. They'd been two of only a handful of freshmen who'd lettered in a sport early enough in the fall to attend the Weekender. He finally found Luker halfway up the hill, wrapped in a long good-bye with Erin.

Nicky batted him with his sleeping bag. "Come on, man, you're going to see her again in five minutes. Let's go claim our bunks." He tried to keep his voice light, but was beginning to get annoyed at his friend's preoccupation.

Stopping to pull a small flashlight from his day pack, Nicky realized he wasn't actually annoyed at Luker. He was jealous. He wished he were saying a temporary good-bye right now to Shana.

The way to his assigned cabin was easy to find with the help of the flashlight. The atmosphere of the musty-smelling, old-fashioned hut made him feel excited as he stepped through the door. It felt as if he were traveling back in time, about to embark upon a great adventure, like a character in some of the old *Hardy Boys* books he used to read.

Claiming a bunk bed in one of the tiny rooms, he tossed his sleeping bag and pack onto the lower bed. He'd make Luker pay for lingering behind by leaving him the top bunk—usually the saggier of the two.

Luker finally appeared, unpacked, then they made their way down the hill toward the main lodge—and a late dinner.

As they jogged down the hill for warmth, Nicky gazed at the sky, bordered on all sides by pointy trees or mountain peaks. The moon was completely covered by clouds, making the steep-walled valley pitch-black. As other students came down the various hills to

14

dinner, their flashlights appeared as pinpoints of light wiggling about in the dark like giant fireflies.

Luker and Nicky burst into the main lodge. Instant bright light, noisy chattering, music, and the smell of wood smoke welcomed them as students bustled about, filling their plates and elbowing their way to tables as close to one of the two huge rock fireplaces as possible. Luker found Erin, then the three of them grabbed turkey sandwiches, apple juice, and oranges, and found an empty corner. Nicky noticed Marta standing alone by one of the fireplaces, searching for a place to sit. He turned the other way.

"Hey!" Erin stood, waving her arm back and forth until she caught Marta's attention. "Here's an empty chair!" Marta gave Erin a thankful smile, worked her way through the crowd, and timidly took the chair next to Nicky.

Thank you, Erin, Nicky said sarcastically to himself.

"Hi, I'm Erin, this is Luker," she said, pointing. "And I think you already know Nicky."

Nicky studied his turkey sandwich as if he'd never seen one before.

"Yes, we met earlier," Marta replied in her squeaky voice, sounding a little formal. "I'm Martinella Lee Prigmore, but my friends call me Marta."

Nicky set his glass of apple juice down a little harder than was necessary and frowned at Marta. "Why don't you drop the speech and just say your name is Marta?"

Erin and Luker looked shocked by his nasty outburst. Marta wrinkled her nose at him, looking as if she was getting used to his temper but was on the verge of not taking his unfriendly comments anymore.

Nicky grabbed his plate, bolted from the chair, and headed across the room. I did it again, he thought. What is it about her that makes me act like a jerk?

15

Why is she nice to me when I'm rude to her? And why can't she be somebody else?

Mr. German and Ms. Egan were clanging knives against their tin cups, trying to get everyone's attention for announcements. Erin saved Nicky's seat, but he leaned against the back wall by himself.

Mr. German, who'd shed his layered clothing, now looked like a lumberjack in a red flannel shirt, blue jean overalls, and a railroad engineer's cap. His booming voice drowned out the last few bits of conversation around the room as he started off with a few weak mountain jokes. Nobody laughed, so he cleared his throat and went on into the announcements. "First the rules," he began. "Curfew is at eleven sharp."

Scruggs started off a round of booing. Mr. German ignored him and continued. "Get a good night's sleep because it's mandatory for everyone to be at the flag salute at seven A.M." The booing turned into groaning.

"Please remember you're in a national forest. Have a healthy respect for the nature around you and stay on the trails. And, dress accordingly. The weather in the high country can change drastically in a matter of a few hours."

Next to Nicky, Scruggs was mimicking Mr. German in a low voice, making the girls around him giggle. Nicky turned his back so he didn't have to watch.

Ms. Egan bounced up on one of the benches and waved her arm for silence. "The scavenger hunt will be the first activity after breakfast, so we'll choose partners tonight. Being ecology-minded, we haven't listed any items that will allow you to harm the natural terrain—no flower picking, branch breaking, etcetera."

Ms. Egan referred to the schedule in her hand, then went on, "Our annual flag football game will start at one, then after that will be our coed softball tournament, and—"

"Destroyers are gonna win!" shouted Scruggs, starting off a chant by his softball team, drowning out Ms. Egan.

Disgusted with Scruggs and the rest of the unfair world, Nicky worked his way toward the back door and quietly slipped out, wanting to be alone. He never took part in the football game, afraid he might injure his knees and ruin his track career. But he did enjoy playing softball. He and Luker made a good combination at shortstop and second base.

Nicky shivered as he climbed the hill to his cabin. Halfway there, he stopped to take in the view of the meadow, visible now that the moon had come out from behind the clouds.

It would make a spectacular photograph, but his camera wasn't equipped to take pictures in dim light. Someday he'd be able to afford one with variable shutter speeds.

The moon was surrounded by hazy grayish rings engulfing broken bits of a rainbow. Nicky remembered a science class discussion about predicting the weather by the appearance of the moon, but now he couldn't recall what the grayish border was supposed to mean. He hoped it meant warmer weather tomorrow.

Continuing his climb, he watched the moon shadows shift across the meadow as the clouds drifted past. After growing up in flat, mountainless country, Nicky always felt a little awestruck at the majesty of the scenery in the mountains. Breathing in the fresh pine scent, he listened to a distant owl hooting somewhere in the darkness and wondered if the owl could sense his presence.

He loved living near the mountains. In the three

17

years he'd lived here, he hadn't actually gotten a chance to do much exploring, but next year he'd be getting his driver's license. After that, he could drive up into the mountains every weekend if he wanted—as long as his dad lent him one of the cars, that is.

Suddenly a hand touched Nicky's shoulder, making him flinch. Startled, he whipped around, fists automatically clenched, expecting Scruggs or one of his punk friends.

The moonlight glinted off the now-familiar glasses as her voice came squeaking out of the darkness. "After you left the lodge, everyone paired off for the scavenger hunt. You and I were the only two without a partner, so Ms. Egan—"

Marta stopped and was quiet, probably hoping for him to respond with enthusiasm.

Nicky sighed instead.

"Here," she finished, her voice falling flat as she shoved the instruction sheet at him. Turning abruptly, she headed toward the girls' cabins.

Nicky watched Marta disappear into the darkness. Part of him wanted to call out to her, offer the use of his flashlight to help find her way in the dark, and maybe learn a little about her. Another part of him was closed to the idea of talking to any girl other than Shana the entire weekend.

The second part won. Nicky hurried on to his cabin. When one thing goes wrong, he mumbled to himself, everything else seems to follow along. He wondered if Marta were thinking the same thing.

Chapter 4

Nicky woke early to run before breakfast. He tried rousing Luker to join him, but his friend would not come to life. Nicky wasn't sure what time Luker and Erin finally said good-bye last night, but he was sure they'd pushed the limits of curfew.

Tugging on a pair of sweats as fast as he could in the ice-cold room, Nicky was tempted to light a fire in the ancient wood stove for the other guys before he left. But the fire would probably burn out before any of them awoke. Instead, he donned a hooded sweat shirt, pulled on his running shoes, and slipped out the door, stopping briefly to stretch since he felt achy from sleeping on the rock-hard bunk bed.

Taking a path he knew led to the lake below the lodge, Nicky was quickly reminded of the high altitude, which made breathing more difficult. The cold air took away his breath and he felt winded before he'd made it halfway down the slope. He slowed, but kept going, then followed the overgrown path around the small lake. The tenseness cramping his shoulders over last night's frustrations began to soften and disappear like the ripples in the lake after a water bug skimmed the surface.

Stopping to walk, Nicky wiped his face on his sweat shirt. It was wet more from the misty rain that had begun to fall than from sweat. The mist seemed to bring out the scent of late-blooming wild flowers, pine needles, and wet wood, making the air heavy and fragrant with the final aromas of a dying forest before it was lost to the frozen winter.

Nicky felt good all of a sudden, rejuvenated, in spite of the dreary overcast sky. Today was a new day. Shana would be here soon. He'd watch for her dad's car, then offer to show her around the camp before any of the other guys did. He hoped she'd get there in time for the softball tournament this afternoon. She'd joined his team last week, so there was no way she could avoid talking to him.

Everyone called it a tournament, even though there were only three teams. It usually took two games, sometimes three, to determine the winner. His team, the Jets, had been practicing hard, motivated more by the urge to wipe out Scruggs' team after all his bragging about how great they were than by the chance to win the coveted Weekender trophy.

With renewed energy Nicky bounded up the hill to his cabin, grabbed a change of clothing, then headed to the building which housed the community showers.

It was during breakfast that he remembered his morning *assignment*—Marta's partner in the scavenger hunt. He wished now he'd said no, but he couldn't because each activity during the Weekender was completed for a grade, and part of the grade was your ability to follow rules and to work as a team.

He'd assumed his partner would be a willing and beautiful Shana, but he'd assumed a lot of things wrong this weekend. Now she'd be paired with another latecomer when she arrived.

Taking his time to enjoy the steaming eggs, hash brown potatoes, crisp bacon, and French toast before

20

him, Nicky remembered how ravenous he became whenever he was in the mountains. He wrapped his hands around a mug of hot chocolate, sipping at it, letting its warmth spread through his insides.

"Ready?" came a voice from behind him. "Ms. Egan just released the list of items we have to collect."

Nicky gulped his hot chocolate until the mug was empty. "Let's go out the back door," he said as he dumped his breakfast tray. "I want to stop by my cabin and get a heavier jacket." He remembered how cold he had been this morning. The frosty wind had whipped right through his jean jacket.

Marta was dressed in hiker's shorts, heavy knee socks, boots, a bulky oversized sweater, and a rain jacket. Strapped to her back was a huge pack, the kind a camper would use on an overnight trek into the back country.

"Come on," Marta urged. "We've got to get a jump on the other kids or all my efforts at being first in line for this list will have been in vain."

Nicky held the door wide, allowing her to maneuver through sideways with her pack. He couldn't believe she was taking it with her on something as simple as a scavenger hunt.

As they climbed the hill to the cabins in the frozen morning air, Nicky realized the main reason he'd brought Marta the back way was so no one would see them leaving together. Under normal circumstances he wouldn't have minded being seen with her. When she looked the other way, he watched her taking long strides up the hill. She looked pretty this morning, especially the way she was dressed. She could've posed for the cover of *Outdoor Magazine*. There wasn't anything wrong with her, he realized. It was just that he didn't want to be linked with another girl before the elusive Shana even arrived.

"Wait here," Nicky ordered, motioning Marta to stop. He flew through the door of his cabin and came to an abrupt halt, surprising Scruggs and a couple of his followers. They all jumped when Nicky burst in on them. Scruggs was trying to hide something. He stuffed it into his jacket pocket.

"Well, if it isn't Nicholas!"

Nicky tensed at the sound of Scruggs' sneering voice.

"Aren't you going on the scavenger hunt, Nicholas?"

Nicky moved toward the tiny room he shared with Luker. "Sure," he replied, forcing his voice to sound casual. "Aren't *you* going?"

"Yeah. Just getting some last minute supplies for my friends here." Scruggs put his arm around one of the guys and they all burst into loud laughter as if they were sharing a private joke.

Grabbing his jacket, Nicky headed toward the door.

"Hey, wait a minute," Scruggs ordered.

Stopping, Nicky glared at them, knowing there was no way he could get the better of all three.

Scruggs stepped close, smelling of beer. "You know that girl your wimpy friend Luker thinks he has exclusive rights to? Well, when I see something I like, I go after it." He glanced out the window where Marta was waiting in plain view. "But I guess you wouldn't know. Not a guy who hangs around with Little Red Riding Hood."

Nicky's face burned. Why did this jerk always leave him tongue-tied, fumbling for something to say? He took a step forward and instantly two of Scruggs' friends reacted, stepping in front to block Nicky's way, like brainless bodyguards they'd seen on T.V.

Anger heated the back of Nicky's neck. He felt as if he was going to explode, unleashing years of hatred and frustration on Scruggs. But he knew before his punches ever reached their target, he'd be flattened by the other two. There was nothing he could do. Turning, he lunged toward the door, unable to get away fast enough as their laughter echoed in his ears.

Chapter 5

"What took you so long?" Marta grumbled as she struggled back into her pack.

"Let's go!" Nicky's words came out like gunshots as he moved ahead of her to hide the angry scowl he knew was smeared across his face. He'd let Scruggs humiliate him again. So what else was new?

"Not that way!" Marta called. "*This* way."

Her angry voice made him stop, whipping around in exasperation.

Off she started up the first hill, stepping over large rocks, trying to keep her balance under the oversized pack.

"Marta!" Nicky snapped. "The trail is the other way."

"That's the path everyone else took while you were in the cabin *forever*." She threw him a disgusted frown. "We wouldn't have a chance of finding anything that way *now*."

Marta dared him with a glare to object. "I explored the hill at six o'clock this morning and I know my way around. I think we can win by going a different direction. The others have gotten a good lead on us so we need to use our heads." She turned her back on him and started hiking. "Follow me." It was more a command than an invitation.

Nicky gave up and followed. If he weren't receiving a grade for his participation this morning, he would have turned around and gone back to bed. He was no more in the mood to go on this stupid scavenger hunt than he was to take a shuttle ride to the moon.

Why was Marta so obsessed with winning? He didn't care one way or the other. He decided to bide his time, let her do all the hunting, then get back to camp as soon as possible. All he wanted was to find Luker and warn him that Scruggs had his eye on Erin, personally rearrange Scruggs' face, then get totally wrapped up in Shana—not necessarily in that order.

To avoid following the well-marked trail everyone else had taken, Marta was leading him straight up the side of the mountain. Sharp pains sliced his lungs with each breath from the steep incline and the altitude. But he was determined to keep up with her. If she could do it, so could he. He was in good shape from track, but then she must be, too, if she were a swimmer like Mr. German had said.

Slowly the hill leveled off and the hiking became easier. Nicky forgot his troubles for a few minutes while he admired the snow-covered peaks above him. The morning dew had formed ice crystals on the surrounding pine trees and buffalo grass. Below him, back toward the lodge, the thin layer of frost coating the meadow was beginning to turn translucent as it melted away. And in his rush he'd forgotten his camera.

The scenery had a calming effect on him. Nicky breathed in the brisk autumn air and began to feel better. Seeing nature in all her glory somehow made him realize the smallness of his own problems.

They hiked in silence for most of the morning. Marta continued leading him in a direction opposite

25

from everyone else. She'd made it clear she knew what she was doing, so he didn't question her.

Each time she found an item from the scavenger hunt list, she'd drop it into a zippered side compartment of the pack. Nicky left her alone, hunting to her heart's content. The sooner she finished, the sooner he could return to camp, get credit for having participated in the activity, then concentrate on enjoying the rest of the Weekender.

His conscience nudged him to help her, but he was afraid to break the silence between them. Talking might lead to another argument. He decided to leave well enough alone.

Hiking without the benefit of a trail was difficult, but being alone in the wilderness had its advantages. They spotted a lot of small animals and even surprised a buck and two does.

Along the way, birds scolded the two with sharp squawks, upset at being startled. They'd make their displeasure known by flapping away with a great rush of wings.

After a while, Marta stopped by a small stream to rest. She took off her pack, pulled out a red bandana, swished it around in the stream, then wiped her face and neck with it.

Nicky watched, feeling annoyance rising in him again, like sap in a budding tree. "What are we stopping for? Let's keep moving." He didn't have any time to waste.

"Look, Nicky Brooks!" Marta yelled as she jumped to confront him, her face turning as red as the bandana. "Quit griping at me! You haven't helped at all so far; you haven't even said two words to me today other than 'you're going the wrong way'." Her voice squeaked with sarcasm. "You're really a fun guy to be

26

with, you know it?'' She flicked the wet bandana in the air like a whip.

Nicky sighed and plopped on a rock to rest. He took a long look at Marta, who'd finished her lecture and had gone back to washing her hands in the stream. She looked like a real mountain girl. And he couldn't help but notice her shapely legs.

Why am I being so hard on her? he asked himself. She's different. But she's nice—and she puts up with me. He laughed out loud.

"What are you laughing about?'' Marta pulled grapes from the pack and pitched them at him as if she was throwing darts at a dartboard.

Nicky caught the grapes in mid-air with one hand. "You have freckles on your legs.'' He watched color creep from her neck to her forehead and felt pleased he'd made her blush.

She looked the other way. "So what?''

Popping some grapes into his mouth, Nicky suddenly felt like a jerk for the way he'd been behaving. He'd been harassing Marta the same way Scruggs always harassed him—only not with as much malice.

Nicky ran a hand through his hair, damp from the morning mist. He hadn't been himself around her at all. No wonder she was yelling at him; he deserved it.

"Hey,'' he said softly to get her attention. She wouldn't look at him, but he went on anyway. "I'm sorry for the way I've been treating you. It's nothing personal. You just happened to be in the wrong place at the wrong time.'' He paused for a moment. "I've been upset about a couple of things and I'm taking them all out on you.'' He picked up a piece of pink granite, tossed it into the clear, cold stream, and watched it sink.

"So I noticed.'' She glowered at him, shading her

eyes from the sun, which was playing hide and seek among the dark clouds. "I was giving you a second chance, but you're blowing it."

He felt relieved she was at least talking to him. "I'm sorry again." He stood and brushed crumpled yellow leaves off his jeans. "What can I do to help?"

"Well, first of all, you could carry the pack part of the time. It's heavy you know, and you could—"

"Wait a minute," Nicky interrupted, hearing his voice rise with annoyance once more. "Why'd you bring this humongous pack on a little scavenger hunt in the first place? I didn't even bring my day pack."

Marta tied the damp bandana to the frame of the pack, wringing excess water out of the ends. "I do a lot of hiking, and it's good to travel light. But it's also handy to take along certain supplies in case you need them. Plus," she added, shooting an impish glance at him. "I just got this for my birthday and wanted to try it out."

"So, what all have you got in there?"

"A first aid kit, food, warm-ups, jeans. A hat, gloves, and a scarf in case it gets colder. An extra jacket, matches, things like that. Plus, it's a place to carry all the items we find."

"Marta, this is a game. We're not climbing Pikes Peak, you know." Nicky yanked up the sleeves of his jacket, then knelt by the stream and scooped water into his cupped hands.

Instantly, Marta grabbed him by the collar and yanked him backwards, making him fall hard onto his elbows. "What are you doing?" she exclaimed.

Startled, Nicky stared up at her, confused. "I was trying to get a drink of water. What's the big deal?"

"Here." She pulled a plastic quart container from her pack and filled it with water from the stream. Then she took out a small bottle of pills and dropped one in. Screwing the cap on, she shook it a couple of times. "Wait a few seconds, then you can have a drink."

Nicky rose slowly, rubbing his elbows. All I want is a drink of water. What are those?" He motioned toward the pills.

She laughed at his reaction, shaking her hands in the air to dry them.

Nicky's insides tightened automatically at the laughter directed toward him. What had he done that was so darn funny?

Marta tossed him the bottle of tiny pills. "These are iodine tablets to purify the water so you can drink it. Read the label if you don't believe me." She gave the bottle another shake. "If I hadn't stopped you, by tomorrow you'd be so sick you'd never want to go hiking again. Pure Rocky Mountain spring water isn't pure at all. It's full of bacteria."

"Really?" Nicky read the label, impressed with Marta in spite of himself.

"How could you not know that if you live so near the mountains?" She cocked her head to study him.

"I've only lived here a few years. There are no mountains—or mountain streams—where I grew up." Nicky kicked himself for not being as informed as he should about surviving in the mountains, even though he was an adopted Coloradan. But other than Chautauqua, his only other jaunts to the mountains had been short day trips to shoot rolls of film whenever it fit into his parents' schedules to drive him.

Taking the bottle from Marta, he held it up, noting its orange tint, then pulled off the cap, and drank. "It tastes funny," he said, wiping his mouth on the arm of his jacket.

"A little. But it's better than getting sick, isn't it?"

29

Nicky regarded her with new respect. "Jeez, you're a walking encyclopedia on mountain survival." He took another swig of water, still watching her as she rearranged the items she'd collected in the pack.

They sat together, leaning against a pile of rocks to eat more grapes and share the purified water in silence while the midday sun softened the tension between them. Nicky was now torn between his urge to hurry and his desire to stretch his time with Marta. Everything new he discovered about her surprised him. "Did you learn all this from that book you were reading on the bus?" he asked.

"Some. My grandparents were forest rangers, so my family spent a lot of summers camping in the Appalachian Mountains. My grandparents loved living and working in the national parks so much, they hated coming to the city—even to visit their grandkids. So we had to go to the mountains to visit them. I guess their love for the wilderness rubbed off on me."

Nicky leaned close as she told him about her camping adventures—once outsmarting a flash flood—owling with her grandfather, and nursing an injured antelope back to health. Her freckle-brown eyes lit up with excitement as she talked, casting a spell over him. He could have listened to her all afternoon.

But it was she who broke the spell, standing abruptly and yanking up her hiker's socks. "We'd better get moving," she said, glancing at the sky.

"Yeah, nothing like taking an hour-long break," Nicky added, rising quickly to stretch, hoping she hadn't noticed his disappointment when she'd ended their conversation.

As they prepared to leave, Nicky's feelings of urgency about returning to Chautauqua returned in a rush, in spite of Marta's company. He helped her shove the water bottle back into a side compartment of the pack. "Let me carry this for a while," he said, thinking he could move faster under the weight of it than she could.

He hoisted it over one shoulder. "Anything else you want me to do?"

"Yeah, now that you've asked. You could help look for the items on the list since that's what we're supposed to be doing. I've done it all so far."

"You got it, Ms. Walking Encyclopedia. What should I look for?"

Marta pulled the list from her pocket. "We still need to find evidence that people have been here, and—"

"Stop. Here you go." Nicky knelt and picked up the stem from the grapes he'd just eaten and tossed aside. "Evidence that people have been here. Go on."

Marta groaned at him. "We can't use something we put here. That's against the rules. And besides, we have to carry out our own garbage."

As she started to drop the stem into the pack, Nicky caught her hand. "This isn't garbage; it's biodegradable. If we leave this stem behind, it might help a bird build its nest someday."

"You're right." She smiled as if pleased they were finally beginning to agree on something. "Ashes to ashes."

"Dust to dust," Nicky finished for her, flinging the grape stem into the bushes. He felt as if he'd scored a major point by coming up with something Marta hadn't thought of. How was a guy supposed to impress a girl who already knew everything? "Let's get going," he said, acting on his new sense of authority.

Feeling refreshed as they started off again, Nicky was actually starting to have fun. But after another half hour, a sudden feeling of uneasiness crept over him

31

like the lengthening shadows. The top of every rise seemed to dip into a new hidden valley, with yet another hill to climb on the other side. Each time he was sure they were on their final descent into the Chautauqua Valley, the terrain would mysteriously deceive him.

And why hadn't they run into anyone else all day? He reasoned it was because they'd taken off in a different direction, avoiding the regular trails. Still, he'd feel much better if they stumbled across a group from camp. At least they could all find their way back together.

Nicky hiked on, listening to the wind rustling in waves through the pine trees, now feeling relaxed with Marta. It was the same sort of feeling Erin's presence gave him. Maybe it was because they hadn't met under normal circumstances, but he felt as if he'd known Marta for a long time instead of less than twenty-four hours. He also decided her squeaky voice and braces made her unique.

Nicky tugged up his jacket sleeve to look at his watch, but it wasn't there. He must have left it in the shower room. Even without the watch, he knew the flag football game must be well under way by now back at Chautauqua, meaning others had already finished the scavenger hunt.

Glancing at the sun, he guessed it was mid-afternoon and wished he hadn't forgotten his watch. Actually he didn't need a watch or the sun to tell him he'd missed lunch. He could tell by his stomach.

Marta suggested they stop to eat a snack she'd smuggled out of the kitchen this morning. As she pulled a thin, ragged blue blanket from the pack and spread it on the ground, Nicky felt irritated again—and suspicious. Marta seemed to be stalling. But why?

32

He'd rather eat while they hiked, to hurry things up, but he joined her on the blanket instead, not wanting to cause any more friction between them.

Quickly they shared a few hard rolls, fruit, and the rest of the purified water, then got ready to move again.

The wind was getting much colder, but Nicky hadn't noticed it until they'd stopped to eat. He began to worry about being late for the softball tournament.

Marta was still taking her time, continuing the hunt.

Nicky jammed his hands into his jacket pockets, trying to think of tactful ways to hurry her up. "Look, we're never going to find the rest of the stuff on the list, and I'm sure we've lost the hunt by now. Let's head back. I can't be late for the softball tournament." The thought of Shana skimmed across his mind, and he wondered if she were at the football game right now.

Marta hesitated. "Can we go a little further? All we have left to find is some kind of footprint, then draw it on notebook paper."

"A footprint would have been easy to find if we'd followed the other kids up the trail like I suggested," Nicky grumbled. He stamped his boot in some soft dirt. "Here, use mine."

She gazed up at him, ignoring his suggestion. "I'll bet no one else has found everything yet." Her pleading eyes unnerved him. "Five more minutes?"

Nicky relented against his better judgement. More than five minutes passed and they still hadn't found a footprint. The sun had long since disappeared for the last time behind angry-looking clouds. Nicky's ears were beginning to freeze, and he thought he felt a snowflake graze his cheek.

A vague sensation of alarm began to gnaw at him.

He tried again to figure out what time it was by the position of the sun, but storm clouds had covered it so thickly, he couldn't quite make out where it was. "*Marta*, we've got to turn back *now!*" He tugged at the zipper of his jacket with freezing fingers.

An unreadable expression clouded her face. Before Nicky could figure it out, she brightened. "I know. We can circle back another way and maybe find the remaining items on the return trip."

Nicky would rather have returned the way they'd come, but since he and Marta had finally started getting along, he wanted to keep it that way. Reluctantly he agreed.

Hiking on this part of the hill was more difficult. Rocks and underbrush were thicker here. They took turns carrying the pack, but both were getting tired from walking for so many hours.

"We should come across one of the trails pretty soon," Marta called. Enthusiasm had returned to her voice. "It will take us straight back to the lodge." Nicky noticed her knees were beginning to turn a little blue.

"It's just up ahead," she hollered. They both started running side by side, partly to keep warm and partly in anticipation of getting to a trail that would take them back to camp and warmth and food.

Nicky and Marta laughed at each other's attempts to run smoothly across the steep rocky slope. Dodging mountain cactus bushes and a few large boulders blocking their pathway, they finally arrived out of breath at the top of the rise.

Their smiles quickly froze on their faces. Snow was definitely beginning to fall, and there before them, the ground fell sharply away in a sheer cliff.

Chapter 6

"Great," Nicky said in a dull voice. "Just great. Okay, Mountain Girl, didn't you say this was the way back?"

"I . . . I think I made a mistake." Marta looked devastated. "I guess I got too wrapped up in the scavenger hunt when I should have been watching where we were hiking." Making a fist, she punched at the air. "Having you mad at me all morning didn't help my concentration, either." She glanced at him, then sighed, as if she were sorry she'd said it. "I didn't mean that, Nicky. I'm not trying to blame you. It's my fault. Go ahead and yell at me." She lowered her eyes, accepting his anticipated reaction.

Even though he felt like yelling, Nicky put his head in his hand instead, trying to hide his disappointment. "Well, we don't have time for you to be sorry," was all he could think to say. "We'd better head back the way we came." His head shot up as the next thought struck him. "You *do* know the way we came, don't you?"

"Sure," Marta replied, a bit feebly. She let the pack slide from her back. "Would you wait a minute while I put on some long pants? My legs are freezing." She dug a pair of sweat pants from the pack, then sat on a rock to unlace her boots.

Nicky felt uncomfortable watching her, even though she was merely pulling sweats on over her hiking shorts. He turned his back and scanned the dense forest for a landmark that might look familiar. Why am I blaming her? he thought. I should have been watching the way we came. He shivered, angry at himself for having no idea where they were or which direction to go.

Nicky remembered last weekend when Luker had borrowed his dad's car and they'd gone to the mall. They'd been so engrossed in a conversation about their upcoming track meet, they hadn't paid any attention to where he'd parked. When it was time to leave, he and Luker spent a half hour trying to find the car. Nicky had been convinced someone had stolen it, and wondered how they could tactfully break the news to Luker's father. But finally it turned up—right where they'd left it. Maybe the way back to camp would come to him eventually, too, if he just concentrated hard enough.

After Marta finished lacing her boots, they hiked down the slope they'd just run up, trying to walk a little too fast and stumbling on the loose rocks. Trudging along in silence, each searched for the trail they thought they'd just missed along the way.

A slow, chilly hour passed. Still they didn't cross a trail or recognize anything that looked even vaguely familiar. The falling snow had mysteriously changed the appearance of the forest. Monstrous flakes fell, thick and heavy. The snow stuck to the ground, rapidly covering up their footsteps. Nicky wished he hadn't let the situation get out of his control. He shouldn't have depended on Marta to lead the way.

"Let's stop for a few minutes," she commanded as they came to a large, snow-splattered rock.

"What? Are you crazy?" Nicky shot back. "We've got to get out of here—the sooner, the better." He tried to hold down the panic he felt rising inside of him as fast as the temperature was dropping. "We don't have time to stop."

"Nicky, we haven't eaten anything since our snack at noon. It's getting late; we need food and water. And," she added, giving him a sidelong glance, "thanks to me, we have some."

She wasn't gloating, he noticed, merely making a point in her favor and trying to smooth over her mistake.

"Besides," she continued, "it seems a lot colder all of a sudden. I think we should take time to put on all the clothes I brought in the pack."

"Put *on* clothes?" Nicky repeated, hearing his voice crack. He hated it when his voice cracked. "My hands and feet are freezing, but the rest of me is burning up from all this exercise. I was just thinking about taking off my jacket."

"No, you can't," she insisted. "We're in danger of getting hypothermia. If you take off your jacket, your body temperature will drop faster than if you leave it on."

Marta lowered the pack to the ground and opened the main compartment. "Haven't you ever read newspaper articles about people dying of exposure in the mountains?"

Nicky shrugged.

"Well, dying of exposure means dying of hypothermia. They probably didn't even know it was happening to them. I once read about a girl who died only ten feet from her house as she was trying to get home without a coat in a sudden snowstorm."

"Terrific," Nicky mumbled. "Everything has gone

wrong this weekend, and now I'm going to die." He brushed snow from the rock and plopped upon it. "Yes, folks, I'm going to die up here on this mountain with a girl who can quote aloud by memory from a book called *Tips on Backpacking and How to Survive.*" He groaned, falling backwards into a thicket of tall grass already wet with snow.

Marta rushed to him, looking alarmed. "Nicky, don't get any wetter than you have to." She pulled him up by his jacket sleeve, as if that might keep him drier. "This is *serious.*" She frowned as he grinned at her.

Now ignoring him, she returned to the backpack to inventory the supplies she'd brought. "I only have one hat, but you can wrap my wool scarf around your head. Most of a person's body heat is lost through the head, you know. And wool repels water."

Marta paused, pulling more articles of clothing out of the pack. "I do have two pairs of gloves, thankfully. One wool pair and one pair of down mittens. We can trade off if we have to, since the down mittens are warmer, and—"

"Stop being my mother!" Nicky snatched the scarf from her hand and wrapped it around his head, knowing he probably looked stupid, but also knowing everything Marta had said was right. Why did it make him so mad that she was right?

After they'd put on all the clothes, Marta unwrapped two turkey sandwiches she'd saved from dinner the night before, but split only one between them in case they needed the other one for later. Nicky thought she was being overly cautious. Surely they'd be home before they needed more food, and right now half a sandwich did little to satisfy his hunger. She wanted to ration the granola bars, too, but he convinced her to split one with him for energy.

38

After their scant meal, Nicky dug out the water bottle, only to remember they'd finished it off earlier. He wasn't thirsty until Marta related another story about a hiker who died from dehydration even though he had a canteen full of water slung over his shoulder. He hadn't felt thirsty either, Marta had said, so he hadn't bothered to keep drinking—a fatal mistake.

That convinced Nicky to scoop snow into the container since there wasn't a stream in sight. He positioned the bottle so heat from his body would help melt the snow. And he dropped in another iodine tablet because he wasn't sure if water from snow was any purer than water from a stream.

Nicky silently refused to ask Marta about it. She'd only make him feel more stupid by knowing the correct answer.

Scrunching a handful of snow into a ball, he bit into it, wondering what it would taste like if it were polluted.

"Nick-eee." Marta's voice sounded tired.

"What?" He took another bite, letting the snow melt into water and trickle down his throat. "Why can't we just eat the snow? It's a lot easier than trying to melt it."

"It's easier, but snow by itself actually dehydrates your body." Marta took off her ski cap to brush wet frizzy bangs out of her eyes, then pulled the cap on again. "Plus, unmelted snow lowers your body temperature, which will bring on hypothermia even faster."

Nicky groaned at her textbook answer. "Sorry I asked." He tossed the rest of the snowball aside, then tugged at the gloves she'd given him, which were warm, but too small. "How smart of me to get lost in the company of a know-it-all."

39

"I have another story about a mother who melted snow in her mouth for her baby while they were snowbound, but then ate the unmelted snow herself. The baby lived but she died."

"I don't think I want to hear it."

"Too late, that's the whole story." Marta readjusted the lighter pack to fit herself.

Nicky reached to help her. "Don't you know any funny stories? Everyone in your stories ends up dead at the end."

He meant it to be a joke, but she gave him a solemn look instead of a smile. "I don't want you to underestimate nature."

"How can I with you around?"

Still no smile.

"Come on, Marta. Lighten up. We're supposed to be having fun. It's a scavenger hunt, remember?"

"It'll seem more like fun later when we're safe and warm and dry." She finally managed a smile. "Come on, partner, let's go home."

Nicky hiked in silence over the slippery, wet rocks, unable to shake Marta's bleak stories from his mind. He was impressed with her ability to stay calm considering their present circumstances. He knew other girls who'd be in hysterics by now, or mad because their make-up was streaking or their hair was getting wet. He never understood why girls acted so upset whenever their hair got messed up.

He was also impressed that Marta could read a book on backpacking and survival, then recall all the important facts when she needed them—so he told her so. "If only I could do that in World History," he added, "I'd be making an *A* instead of a *C*. Sometimes my mind goes blank after I've read the assignment, and I can't even remember what I just read." She laughed at

40

him, so he threatened her playfully with a glove full of snow.

"It helps if you're interested in the subject."

"You're right. Ask me anything about famous track stars and I'll bore you for an hour with the answer."

"I'll pass, thank you."

The small talk had temporarily taken Nicky's mind off how dark the forest was becoming. He squinted at the area around them, trying not to take deep breaths because the cold air stung his nostrils. "I doubt all the sports trivia in the world can get us out of here," he mumbled more to himself than to Marta.

The calmness of the falling snow seemed to mock the anxiety bubbling in Nicky's chest. As his eyes watered from the cold air, he blinked to focus on the late afternoon sky, now a mean-looking shade of dark gray.

The forest seemed magical and enchanted. Nicky half expected to see wood nymphs and fairies dancing around the trees as they did in folktales. Yet he couldn't enjoy the beauty of the scenery anymore, with or without his vivid imagination.

The wind had died down, making the forest still and quiet—too quiet for Nicky's comfort. In West Texas, stillness always preceded a tornado. He knew he was in no danger of tornados here, yet the stillness touched a deep instinct, warning him to be on guard.

Nicky glanced at Marta, struggling under the weight of the pack over her bulky clothes. He knew she was trying to be brave, but she looked so small against the backdrop of giant pines, looming high like Christmas trees with their pointed tops and heavy sprinkling of snow. Nicky felt a surge of protectiveness wash over him, and he wanted to reassure her.

He realized it was just as much his fault they were

41

lost as it was hers. It wasn't fair of him to let her take the blame upon her shoulders. At least she'd thought about rationing the food, getting more water, and making sure they both had enough clothing on to keep warm—things he never would have considered. He was more inclined to bound off, spontaneous and unprepared, searching for a trail—and not stopping until he found one.

"Come here." He hadn't meant his voice to sound as gruff as it did. "Let me carry the supplies for a while." Nicky lifted the pack from her shoulders and leaned it against a tree, then awkwardly reached to brush snow from Marta's hair, which seemed longer now that it was wet. Her hair tangled through his fingers as he tried to smooth it.

Instinctively, his arms went around her. She let herself be pulled into his embrace, returning the hug.

Her hat slipped off, but Nicky caught it before it fell into the snow. "We're in this together, Martinella Lee Prigmore," he whispered into her hair, "and we're going to come through it together. Okay?"

"Okay," she agreed faintly, her squeaky voice muffled by his jacket.

They kept hugging for a long, long time in the silent, darkening forest before Nicky collected the backpack and they slowly trudged off again.

Chapter 7

"It's getting too dark to see." Marta's voice was barely more than a tired mumble.

Nicky'd been thinking the same thing as he stumbled over hidden rocks in the darkness, but hadn't wanted to mention it. His mind had refused to entertain the thought that he might not be warm and safe, sleeping in his cabin at Chautauqua before dark—and laughing with Luker over the events of this strange day. Saying out loud that night was catching up with them was—in his mind—giving up. It was admitting they were lost, without a doubt, and might as well accept the fact they would not find their way back to camp until morning.

"We'd better start scouting for a place to take cover." Nicky thought that seemed the right thing to say even though he didn't know what to scout for, other than a Holiday Inn. But he assumed Marta would have an opinion or two on the subject.

After much searching in the dim light, they found a hollowed-out area surrounded by giant boulders. One lone, flat rock jutted overhead, creating something of a roof. It wasn't exactly a cave, but it was better than nothing.

Marta unzipped a small compartment in the pack, and pulled out a flashlight. Stooping slightly, she tiptoed into the area, swinging the light back and forth.

It created eerie shadows against the back wall. "I hope this isn't the home of a wild animal," she whispered as if someone or some*thing* were listening. "This seems too good to be true."

They held the circle of light in front of them, and searched the ground for bones, footprints, or other signs of animals, but found none. They did find litter and ashes from previous fires, indicating the shelter had been used as a campsite. It reassured Nicky to think other people had already been here. They must not be too far out in the wilderness after all.

He dropped to his knees, ready to accept the shelter as home for the night. "We're out of the snow, but it's still colder than a skating rink in here."

Marta continued to explore. "It looks as if campers have built fires right outside the entrance." She fanned the flashlight back and forth above the shelter. "We can try a fire, too, but we'll have to set it as far to the left as we can."

"But there's already a circle of rocks on the right." Nicky was too tired to argue. Why was she making more work out of it than was necessary? "And the trees hang over there," he added, moving to the makeshift rock fireplace. "If we build the fire here, the trees will block the falling snow and keep it from going out." His logic sounded good to him.

Marta was already moving the rocks in spite of his logic. "You shouldn't build a fire under a tree, no matter how wet the weather is. It only takes a spark to—"

"Start a forest fire," he finished for her. So much for his logic. Why hadn't he thought of that? Nicky mentally kicked himself as he helped her move the rocks to form a new circle.

She scooped snow from the middle of the area. "I

might add that the heat would melt snow on the branches, making it drip into the fire and put it out.''

Nicky tried to ignore the let-me-handle-it look on her face. If they depended on his irrational logic, they'd probably be dead by morning. He jammed a rock into the ground, splattering mushy snow onto his jeans. Why did she always have to win?

Marta gave him a sly look. ''Speaking of fires, it's a good thing one of us remembered to bring matches.''

He shifted the last rock into place. ''Go on, rub it in.'' He wasn't angry at her. He was angry at himself for being so stupid.

Nicky cleaned the mud off his gloves by scraping them against the rock wall of the shelter. ''You win, Marta. I'm glad you were crazy enough to bring all these supplies with you on a measly little scavenger hunt.'' He expected a smug look from her, but instead, she lowered her eyes and turned the other way.

The words *scavenger hunt* lingered in Nicky's mind. It seemed like some game they'd played in another lifetime. All of a sudden it wasn't a game anymore. He glanced around at their bleak surroundings, feeling as if they'd set out from Camp Chautauqua years ago, instead of hours ago.

''Okay, Girl Scout, I've got a new problem for you.'' Nicky realized he was deliberately trying to think up problems she wouldn't know how to deal with—just to see her crumble. Why couldn't she act helpless and cry for a change? A lot of other girls he knew would react that way. Why'd she have to act so darn confident? Pulling on his wet gloves, he watched her face. ''How are you going to start a fire with wet wood?''

She handed him the flashlight. ''Look behind that ledge on the right.''

45

Nicky investigated the wall he hadn't bothered to look at before. A thick rock ledge created a backward slanted shelf. Neatly piled in the crook of the ledge was a small stack of dry logs, left behind by a thoughtful picnicker.

"This is too easy," he said. "Something's bound to go wrong." As he danced the flashlight around the walls, looking for other ledges, it came to him. "Ah-ha, there isn't enough wood here to last through the night. We'll be frozen as solid as these rocks by morning."

"No we won't. Come on."

"What do you mean, come on?" Nicky shone the light into Marta's face. She'd taken off her ski hat, which had left her wet hair plastered to her head. It wasn't very becoming, but then he guessed his hair probably looked the same way underneath the wool scarf. "I'm not leaving this shelter. I'm going to sit down, relax, and call Maxie's pizza delivery." Plopping against a rock, Nicky grinned up at her. "See if the evening paper's arrived yet, my dear."

Marta shook out her hat and pulled it back on, stuffing wet ends of her hair underneath. "Yes, you are leaving this shelter—for a little while, at least. We have to bring in more firewood so it can dry out. If we're lucky, we'll find some that hasn't gotten too wet by now."

It took a lot of effort for Nicky to get to his feet. His conditioning for track hadn't prepared him for walking, mostly uphill, hours and hours on end. His legs ached from overuse, and his arms and back were sore from the heavy pack. If Marta hadn't been right about collecting more wood, nothing would have made him get to his feet again. Except for the fact that she was still on her feet.

Marta grabbed the pack. "We can put smaller pieces of kindling in the top," she explained to Nicky's questioning glance, "and carry the larger pieces in our arms. It might save us a trip or two."

He followed her outside as she continued her lesson.

"My grandfather always said to collect all the wood you think you'll need for the night, then double that amount, and you might have enough. Plus, we need to find a few big logs to pile up against the rocks behind the fire so they can reflect heat back into the shelter. They can be wet because we don't want them to burn."

Nicky was only half-listening as he stumbled down the slope to the trees, but Marta's calm voice was soothing. The way she was logically handling their situation reassured him they were doing the right thing. He was too tired to think—logically or illogically. He wouldn't have bothered with a fire tonight. He would've curled up in the shelter and slept. Yet something in the back of his mind reminded him that you shouldn't let yourself fall asleep if you're in danger of freezing to death.

Marta leaned the pack against the white trunk of an aspen tree and turned off the flashlight. The snow-white surroundings allowed them to see well enough without the light.

She showed him how to find dry kindling underneath wet logs and rocks, and how to break off dead branches kept dry by those above them. He piled a stack of kindling neatly under a pine tree, then continued to scout around, kicking at stumps, and turning over logs. A few minutes later, he couldn't find the wood he'd stacked. Between the dim light and the sameness of the falling snow, it was easy to get disoriented. It unnerved him a little, so from then on, Nicky

47

kept one eye on the entrance to the shelter, trying not to think what would happen if he got lost from that. He would never survive the night without some kind of protection—and Marta's supplies. And Marta herself, he added.

By the third trip out, their spirits had lifted. Nicky staged a one-sided snowball fight with Marta, who couldn't return the fire because her arms were full of wood. They found themselves laughing together for the first time in hours. For the first time—period.

Even though everything had gone wrong since the Weekender had started—*really* wrong—Nicky added to himself, he liked Marta, even though she aggravated him every five minutes. But he couldn't help thinking how much more he'd be enjoying their little adventure if only he knew his dad would be driving up any minute to give them a ride home.

Nicky tried not to think about his dad or his mom, as he wandered further into the night. Surely they'd been notified by now that their son had disappeared from Chautauqua. Along with the new girl in school— ha. That might be good for his reputation with the guys, but not with his family. Still, he felt sorry for putting his parents through a night of worry. Especially after they'd been harping on him to be more responsible.

He vowed to make it up to them when he got home—helping around the house, shoveling the walks without being asked—whatever it took to show them he *was* responsible.

Nicky got so caught up in his owns thoughts as he searched for firewood, he jumped when an arm brushed against his. Hope skittered through his mind that it was someone coming to their rescue, but it was only Marta, smiling up at him in the white night, a dark smudge of dirt across one cheek.

"Isn't this *almost* fun?" She laughed.

"It's the most *almost* fun I've had all day." He grinned back, reacting with a sudden overwhelming urge to kiss her. The urge surprised and unsettled him at the same time as they stood gazing at each other. Shana was the girl he was crazy about. No one else.

Nicky sensed danger at the same moment Marta did. As if on cue, both spun around at the same instant, then froze. A dark form that hadn't been there moments before moved among the shadowed pines.

Nicky wanted to run, but his feet wouldn't obey. All his strength evaporated in fear. Marta let the wood fall from her arms. It clunked to the ground, drawing unwanted attention in their direction. She grabbed Nicky's hands, jerking him down into a squatting position.

He twisted away from her. "Run to the shelter!" His war cry came out as a hoarse whisper. And even as he yelled it, he knew the shelter would be no protection from what was eyeing them in the distance.

She held tightly to his hands, jerking him down a second time. "Be quiet! Don't move a muscle!" Sliding her arms around his neck, she pulled his cheek next to hers so she could whisper into his ear. "Please, if we run, it will chase us like a wild dog. If we stay calm and still, it *should* leave us alone." Her voice was shaking so badly, Nicky could hardly understand the words.

He obeyed. She'd been right about everything else so far; why should he doubt her now? He remained frozen in this awkward position, his arms grasping

49

Marta, her knees clenched between his. What a way to die, was all he could think.

In the stillness of the falling snow, the huge black bear reared up on its hind legs, sniffed the frigid air, then lumbered straight toward them.

Chapter 8

Nicky followed the shadowed form of the bear with his eyes, until the animal moved beyond his line of vision. He didn't turn his head, afraid it might attract the bear's curiosity. His heart even refused to beat for fear the bear could hear it.

Holding his breath, Nicky prayed for the obvious—that the animal was merely passing by. Then he heard it growling and ripping into something. The backpack! Their food! The bear had been attracted more by the scent of the turkey sandwich than by their human scent. Nicky was relieved, yet scared about losing what food they had. Feeling brave, he raised his head to look.

Marta tightened her hold on him. "Stay still," she hissed. "Let him take our food and hope that's all he wants."

Nicky's heart seemed to pound in his ears. He could barely hear Marta's words. He shuddered to think what might have happened if the bear had appeared after they'd fallen asleep in the shelter with the pack and the food lying between them.

They remained huddled together long after the noises had stopped, until Nicky's legs started to ache. Finally he dared a glance. "He's gone." Both collapsed backwards in relief, not caring if they got wet from the snow. "You go back to the shelter," Nicky ordered, wanting to be in charge. "I'll get what's left of our supplies."

Marta started to protest.

"Go." He nudged her up the hill, now feeling embarrassed that the bear had scared him so much. Did Marta think he was a coward? What if the animal had attacked? Would he have been able to protect her? Or himself? As always, she was the one who'd known what to do.

By the time Nicky gathered everything the bear had tossed around and carried the pack up the hill to the shelter, Marta had piled the larger logs outside the circle of rocks, creating a crude heat reflector.

With a knife from the pack, he helped her cut three large evergreen boughs. Holding the flashlight, he watched her erect a tall, y-shaped stick in the middle of the fire circle, securing it with a few heavy rocks. Then she removed the shoelaces from her boots and used them to tie the evergreen boughs onto the stick, creating a makeshift umbrella over the fire circle to protect it from the falling snow.

"The green boughs will make the fire smoke a lot, but we don't have a choice," she said, answering his unasked question. "Without their cover, the fire will die."

Nicky collected litter scattered about the cave and combined it with a few dead branches. He now knew what the expression *chilled to the bone* meant because that's exactly how cold he felt. He wished Marta would hurry with the fire.

She was sorting through her pockets. "I don't have enough matches. Can you bring me more from the pack?" She glanced up at him. Her pale smudged face looked ghostly in the dim light from the flashlight.

Nicky had secretly been counting on Marta having

extra matches in her pocket. His heart sank at her words. "They're gone," he said in a quiet voice. "Ruined. The bear scattered them in the snow." He watched her face for a moment. "If we can't start a fire, we'll never survive the night, will we?" He tried to keep his voice steady so she wouldn't know he was afraid. But there was no point in ignoring the obvious. Whether or not the temperature was cold enough to kill them, the chill factor was deadly. All they had to do was fall asleep, then they'd never wake up. At least it sounded like a painless way to die.

"We're not going to die. Hand me the flashlight."

She grabbed the light and started off down the hill, back to where the contents of the pack had been scattered.

Nicky followed, not questioning her actions anymore. He felt jumpy knowing the bear was around, lurking somewhere behind a boulder or a tree, watching them like a monster in a horror movie.

He tried to be patient, but the temperature seemed twenty degrees colder out here than inside the shelter. "Marta, I *told* you I looked for matches. Believe me, they're all wet."

"I'm looking for a film container."

"If the matches were ruined, your film will be ruined, too." Why did she need film now? Had she suddenly lost her good sense? He needed a fire. The sooner the better.

"The container doesn't have film in it. It's for extra matches."

They turned the snow over in handfuls until they found the container. Nicky opened it gingerly. "The matches are still here, but snow leaked in. They're no good either." He snapped the lid on and tossed the container to her. Nicky pulled himself to his feet, reaching for a tree limb to steady himself. He'd never felt this tired—or this cold—in his life. "Come on, let's get back to the shelter. I'm freezing."

He was sorry the instant he said it. Marta hadn't complained once about being cold or tired. He didn't want her to think he couldn't handle the situation. "Are you all right?" he added quickly, wishing she could show a little weakness so he'd stop being impressed by everything she did.

Marta was obviously all right, half-running through the mounting snow as best she could. What was there to act so excited about? he wondered, trudging after her.

Dropping to his knees, he watched as she uncapped the film container. "These matches are special," she said. "I dipped them into a bottle of fingernail polish to seal the tips. They'll work even if they're wet."

"Fingernail polish?" Nicky made a face at her. "*Normal* girls put that on their fingernails, not on their matches."

"I guess I'm not a normal girl."

He laughed at the understatement. "I figured that out *miles* ago, Ms. Prigmore. Now can we *please* get a fire going before I turn into the abominable snowman?"

"Snow*person*." She smirked at him.

He pretended to ignore her correction of his terminology and moved to block the wind as she worked on the fire. Using the litter and pieces of dry branches for tinder, she finally got a small flame going. Nicky tried to pile on a lot of logs to hurry it up, but Marta scolded him about smothering what fire they had. Better to let it build gradually, she said. Nicky held his breath until the tiny flame grew in strength.

The reflector worked well, directing what heat there was towards them. They faced each other, huddling close to the fire, and sorted through the remains of the backpack.

The bear had eaten the last sandwich, fruit, and granola bars. The only food left was a bag of hard lemon drops.

"Terrific," Nicky mumbled, knowing there was no way he could have scared off the bear once it had gotten a whiff of their food. Yet the food seemed a small sacrifice to pay for their lives.

"Don't worry," Marta said. "We can suck on the lemon drops for energy. We've got water from the snow we melted, and we can always melt more." She fanned the fire with a small bough. "I certainly don't think we're in danger of running out of snow."

Nicky followed her gaze to the storm that was definitely picking up momentum. Snow was falling more heavily now, and the wind was beginning to howl. In the glow from the flashlight, it looked like a white wall bordered their shelter, as if they were at the edge of the world.

"I wasn't hungry until our food disappeared," Nicky said, groaning. "Now I'm starved. I think I'll order that pizza from Maxie's with everything on it. I'd even choke down a few anchovies if I had to."

Marta pushed him away. "Hush, you're only making it worse." She gave him a few lemon drops and ate one herself, then carefully folded the package shut and shoved it into her jacket pocket.

Reaching for the pack, she assessed the damage. "I think we can tie this up well enough to carry it on our backs. It's not ripped as badly as it could have been." She felt around in the bottom compartment. "What's this?"

Marta drew out her hand. In it were a few pieces of broken glass. "Oh, my glasses. They're shattered."

"Your glasses? I didn't even notice you'd taken them off. Can you see?"

"They kept getting wet from the falling snow, so I put them into the pack, where I *thought* they'd be safe. I can see well enough without them." Marta gave him a sheepish look. "I got us lost with them on, maybe I'll have better luck getting us out of here with them off."

She upended the pack and shook it until the rest of the broken glass fell out. With a stick, she tried to dig a hole to bury the sharp pieces.

Nicky stayed silent for a few moments, still feeling guilty about letting her absorb all the blame. "Hey." He caught her hand as she scraped at the frozen top layer of dirt. "You didn't get us lost. We both got us lost. I'm not blaming you."

She held his stare. The fire danced in her warm eyes. "You'll blame me when you hear my confession."

"What confession?"

Marta didn't answer. She jabbed the stick into the dirt faster and faster.

Nicky grabbed the stick, flinging it to the back of the shelter. Being ignored exasperated him.

"What confession?" he repeated.

Leaning closer to the fire, she hugged her knees to her chest. "Will you be mad if I tell you?"

"Yeah. I'll be so mad I'll get right up and go home." He sighed. "Look, we're stuck with each other for a while, whether we want to be or not, so there's no point in getting mad or fighting."

"Promise?"

How could one person aggravate him so much? "I promise."

"All right." She took a deep breath. "I've known all day that we were lost."

Nicky stared at her. "What do you mean, all day?"

"Since we stopped the first time to eat."

"You were lost *then?*"

"Well, not exactly lost. Disoriented."

"Why didn't you tell me?"

"You weren't speaking to me."

"Then why didn't you tell me after we started speaking to each other again?" Nicky shifted closer to the fire, still freezing.

"Because." Marta paused, grabbing another stick to poke at the fire. "I couldn't believe that I didn't know where we were. Do you remember the shortcut we took? Up the side of the hill?"

"Yes, I remember. So do my lungs and my legs."

"At the top of the third rise, according to my calculations, we should have intersected the main trail, and cut ahead of half the students who started at the beginning."

"You obviously calculated wrong. Why didn't you ask for my help?"

"Because I was sure I could figure out where we were, get us back on track, and—" She leaned her chin on top of her knees to watch for his reaction, "save face by keeping you from suspecting anything."

It was too late to get mad at her, Nicky reasoned, trying to calm his temper. He'd spent a whole day admiring Marta for her brains and ability, only to find out she'd been leading him on a wild goose chase all day, as his mother would say. Now he understood why she'd kept stalling this afternoon. She hadn't known which direction to go.

"Nicky, I know better than this." She pointed the stick at herself. "I've spent every summer of my life hiking and camping. My grandfather would be so disappointed in me. I can't believe I—"

Nicky raised a hand to silence her. "It's okay," he said, even though that's not the way he felt. He was still angry at himself for not questioning her earlier. "But if you'd just told me, we could have put our heads together and spent the day finding our way back instead of pretending to be on a scavenger hunt."

She winced at his words. "We didn't ask to be partners today. You were already mad about getting stuck with me, so I thought the less said, the better."

Nicky laughed at the irony of the whole situation. The more he and Marta tried to avoid each other, the more they were thrown together. It could have been worse, he thought. He could have been stuck all day with Kelli Tafoya and not had anyone to talk to.

"Well, no use crying over spilt turkey sandwiches." Nicky stretched his sore legs. "And even though our friendship got off to a pretty rocky start . . ." He paused, eyeing their rock shelter, "I'd say it's still pretty rocky."

At last she smiled. "I know we're victims of circumstance, but I'm really not having that terrible of a time with you."

"Was that a compliment?" He wasn't sure whether or not he should feel flattered. "It's not as though you picked me out of all the sophomore guys. I just happened to be the only guy on the bus with an empty seat next to him." He discreetly left the rest of the story untold.

She shrugged. "I meant it as a compliment. I wasn't going to come on the Weekender at all since I didn't know anyone, but Ms. Egan convinced me it'd be a good way to make new friends."

"Getting a guy stranded out in the middle of nowhere is not a good way to make new friends." He playfully wrapped his hands around her neck, pretending to strangle her. "We'll be friends till the end!" he exclaimed. "And this is the end!"

She laughed, pulling away from him. "It's not easy for me to admit I'm wrong."

"So I noticed. You have a winner complex."

Her expression told him she knew what he meant.

Giving up on her plan to bury her broken glasses, she dumped the pieces into a side compartment of the pack, then yanked out the ragged blue blanket they'd picnicked on earlier. Moving beside him, she folded it over their laps.

Nicky watched her pull off the ski hat and comb her fingers through her wet hair, trying to untangle it. The hat had kinked her hair into waves. As she combed it forward in front of her shoulders, her hair caught the light from the fire, looking as though it were the same color. Nicky wanted to touch it.

She noticed him watching, and fidgeted self-consciously. "I don't think we should sleep at the same time—just in case. I doubt the bear will come back though, since we don't have any food left."

"Oh yeah? What about us? To a bear, *we're* food."

Marta grimaced. "I was trying not to think about that." She clicked off the flashlight. "Better save the batteries."

"We should keep the fire going all night," Nicky added, "since we're almost out of matches."

They were silent for a while, both lost in their own thoughts. Nicky wanted to give in to sleep, but felt he should let Marta sleep first. It was a waste of energy to feel angry over her miscalculation. He wished he could say something to make her feel better.

Nicky touched her arm. "Maybe we've been missed by now and they've started looking for us."

She brightened. "Yeah. And I'm sure we'll find our

way back in the morning. As long as we can get through tonight.''

He felt her shiver, so he rearranged the blanket around their shoulders.

''Nicky?'' she whispered. ''When we were out there with the bear, what was going through your mind?''

He hesitated, using the blanket as an excuse to shift his body closer to hers. ''Actually, I was thinking about how nice you smell.''

Marta gave a quick laugh, pulling back to stare at him. ''My whole life is passing before my eyes and you're thinking about how nice I smell?''

He grinned, nudging her with his shoulder. She returned his smile, reaching to arrange his hair. The tenderness of her touch made his heart lurch. He'd never had so many conflicting emotions over one person in his whole life. But he liked the way she was looking at him. And he liked her touch. And he liked—

A sudden noise outside the shelter bolted them both to their feet. Marta grabbed his jacket sleeve, and Nicky instinctively pulled her toward him. Had the bear come back?

They stood stiffly, hardly able to breathe while the noises continued.

''I'll see what it is.'' Nicky's voice was barely a whisper. Marta reached to stop him. For a moment their eyes locked as they shared the same fear.

Nicky's heart was pulled in two directions. Half of him wanted to stay with Marta's warmth, and the other half knew he had to prove to her he could protect them. Prove to her she could feel safe and look to him for answers, too. She'd been protecting him long enough.

Time seemed to stop while his brain tried to convince his legs of the right thing to do. He cupped

Marta's face in his gloved hands and memorized her eyes. Leaning down, he kissed her gently. As her arms went around his neck, he pulled her close, lifting her off her feet in a hug, wanting to kiss her again and again.

Instead, he released her. There would be time for kisses later. After he'd impressed her with his courage. Stepping back, Nicky avoided her eyes, afraid she might read the dread he felt certain was reflected there.

He grabbed a narrow log from the fire to use as a torch—a heroic gesture he'd once seen in a movie. Holding it high in front of his face, he stepped out into the storm.

If the noises were coming from the bear, he reasoned, the fire should scare it away. But in two steps his torch fizzled from the heavy downfall of wet snow. So much for heroic gestures, he thought, gripping the torch anyway as if it were a weapon.

He followed the sounds. They led him about fifty feet from the shelter. There, at the foot of a scraggly pine tree, a person was lying face down in the snow. Nicky's heart thundered inside his chest. Was it a dead body?

Snow was blowing into his eyes, making it impossible to see clearly. He tried to run toward the still form, but the drifts had deepened into the side of the hill. In slow-motion agony he plowed his way through the deepness, knelt, and rolled the body over.

It was Scruggs.

Chapter 9

Marta helped Nicky carry Scruggs into the shelter and place him as close to their paltry fire as possible. "We've got to get his wet clothes off and warm him up *fast!*" Marta exclaimed, going into action. Scruggs was shaking badly and was a little out of his head. He let himself be taken care of.

Nicky hung back, not knowing what to do. He watched Marta struggle to pull Scruggs' snow-crusted jacket off his limp arms. Scruggs, of all people. Just thinking the name gave Nicky a headache. How stupid of him to be out here in the middle of the night with no protection.

As soon as the thought crossed Nicky's mind, he realized they must be as stupid as Scruggs, since they were in the same situation.

"Help me!" Marta snapped him into action. She was fumbling with the buttons on Scruggs' shirt. "We'll have to donate some of our dry clothes, then wrap up with him in the blanket until his body temperature returns to normal." She threw off her own jacket, struggled out of her oversized sweater, then threaded Scruggs' arms through the sweater sleeves.

"What?" Nicky wasn't sure he heard her correctly as he made a half-hearted attempt to help. He couldn't argue with giving up some of his dry clothes, but wrap up with Scruggs in a blanket? No way.

"Nicky, it's a matter of life or death." Marta's voice was somber. "Our warmth will help raise his body temperature. Look at him. He's shaking, and he doesn't even know where he is or what's happening to him. He's in the early stages of hypothermia. Remember what I told you?"

As Marta shook the snow off Scruggs' jacket, something clinked in the pockets. She pulled out two empty beer bottles. "Look! He's crazy. Alcohol affects people faster at this altitude, and—"

"Would you stop with the encyclopedia talk for a minute?" Nicky's voice echoed off the walls of the shelter. He could see for himself how serious Scruggs' condition was, but he didn't need an actual diagnosis from Doctor Prigmore. He grabbed her hands as she struggled with the frozen zipper on Scruggs' jeans. "I'll do that—if it has to be done."

"This is no time to be modest," she answered, but Nicky read her look of relief when he took over. Peeling off a half-dead person's stiff, wet jeans was not easy. Marta gave in to her modesty after all, covering Scruggs with the blanket while Nicky struggled to undress him.

Between the two of them, they re-dressed Scruggs in Marta's warm-up pants, which were much too small, but at least were dry. Marta's heavy jacket went over the sweater she'd already put on him.

The two rolled up in the blanket on opposite sides of Scruggs, rubbing his arms and legs to speed up his circulation. He winced when they rubbed one of his legs, so they assumed he'd been injured. How badly, they couldn't tell.

After a while, he stopped shaking and fell asleep.

"We can't let him sleep," Marta said, "It's too dangerous." She jostled him and talked in a loud voice, nonsense words, just to stimulate his awareness. Her voice soothed Nicky, actually reminding him of nursery rhymes his grandmother used to read to him. Funny, he hadn't thought about that in years.

During the next hour, the fire and body heat did the trick. Scruggs finally opened his eyes, looking confused and suspicious at the same time, but unable to do anything about it, like a rescued bird with an injured wing.

As soon as Scruggs became conscious, Nicky moved far away from him. Marta wrapped the blanket around her patient, then heated a small amount of water in a piece of torn aluminum foil which had held one of the sandwiches. When it became too hot to hold, she poured the heated water into the lid of the plastic bottle.

Struggling, she raised Scruggs' head with one hand and tipped the lid toward his lips with the other. "Here, drink this," she coaxed.

"What . . . is . . . it?" Scruggs's speech was slurred.

"It's hot water to warm your insides."

"Hot . . . water?"

"It's all we have." Marta sounded impatient. "Drink it." She cradled his head in her arm, tilting the lid so he could sip at it.

As Scruggs drank, his eyes traveled from Marta to Nicky and back again. Nicky was jogging in place, swinging his arms to keep warm and to stay awake. He wondered what Scruggs was thinking.

"Who?" he began slowly. "Who *are* you?"

His mind was still in a fog. Nicky rather liked

Scruggs' incapacitated condition. It kept him from insulting Nicky in front of Marta.

"I'm Martinella—" She stopped and glanced at Nicky. "I'm Marta Prigmore and this is Nicky Brooks. You know, from Mitchell High?"

Scruggs squinted at him. "Nicky Brooks?"

Nicky tried to hide his disdain of their intruder from Marta. "Yeah," is all he answered, trying to sound aloof. "We're here because we got caught in the storm and had to take shelter." He left out the part about getting lost. "What are *you* doing out here by yourself?"

He felt Marta's stare, obviously questioning the irritation in his voice.

Scruggs made a few unsuccessful attempts to sit up, so Marta helped. He shuddered and drew closer to the fire. Nicky grabbed more kindling from the back of the shelter, piling it on to keep the flames going. In spite of Scruggs' nearness, Nicky opted to stay close to the warmth.

It was quiet for a long time, until Scruggs' haziness cleared well enough for him to tell his story.

"All I remember is that we—Givan and me—took off on the scavenger hunt. We ran into these two girls, so we told them we'd *help* them with the stupid hunt." He chuckled to himself as he became more alert.

"We got off the trail and into the forest, which is what Givan and I had planned. Then we started to have our own little party. But when we pulled out the beer, the girls acted funny."

His hand automatically moved to his jacket pocket where Marta had found the bottles before he realized he wasn't wearing his own clothes. "You undressed me?" His eyes moved away from Nicky and rested on Marta.

"We had to get you into dry clothes to stop you from shaking." Marta stoked the fire with a stick, avoiding Scruggs' eyes. Nicky wanted to punch the amused look off the jerk's face.

"Get on with your story," he snapped.

Scruggs took another sip of hot water, still watching Marta, which infuriated Nicky. "They were some *fine* looking girls," he continued. "Givan and I drank the beer ourselves, then he wandered off with the brunette, Karen, and I ended up with the blond, Shana. I like ending up with blonds." Scruggs was the only one who laughed at his joke.

The temperature in the shelter seemed to go up two hundred degrees at the mention of Shana's name. Nicky clenched his fists inside his pockets, not wanting to listen to the rest of the story. "Get to the point!" he yelled. "What happened to *you?*"

Marta stopped poking at the fire and stared at him, acting confused by his behavior toward their unwelcome guest. Unwelcome as far as he was concerned.

Scruggs' lack of response to Nicky's nastiness surprised him. Under normal circumstances, one of Scruggs' friends would have flattened anyone who popped off at him. He seemed to be moving in slow motion, as if he were drunk. Nicky figured his reflexes were still dulled from the cold.

"All right, all right," Scruggs said. "I'll skip all the *good* parts." He leered at Marta until she turned away. "I never saw Givan and the other girl again. Shana and I were having a good time—a *great* time, actually— until I stepped out on a ledge, and slipped on some loose rocks. I fell about a dozen feet." He rubbed his bad leg. "Hurt my leg and couldn't walk on it, so Shana left to get help." He pulled Marta's hat off his

66

head and ran his hand through his hair, making it spike up more than usual.

Sighing as if a great weariness was overtaking him, Scruggs went on, "I was all right until it started snowing. The temperature must have dropped a hundred degrees in less than an hour. I tried to drag myself down the hill a ways, looking for protection from the wind. The pain in my leg was getting worse, so I drank more beer to dull it."

Scruggs leaned his head in his hands, scrunching Marta's hat against his forehead. "I . . . I guess I lost track of the time, and where I was going, so if Shana came back, I wasn't where she'd left me."

"Stupid idiot," Nicky mumbled. "You—"

"It *was* stupid of you to move away from the spot where she left you," Marta said, cutting Nicky off. She glanced at him, frowning at his hostility. "But it's over now, and we've got other problems here to deal with."

Scruggs lifted his head from his hands. His face had turned ghostly pale. "She never came back." His tough exterior slipped off like a snake's second skin. "I—I thought I was going to die out there!" He struggled to his feet, but Marta pulled him down.

Nicky felt as if he'd just witnessed Rambo crying. He'd never seen Scruggs act like a human being before, or express any kind of emotion at all—other than obnoxiousness, if that were an emotion.

Marta spoke softly to calm him. She made him lie down, then cradled his head in her lap, comforting him with her nearness.

Nicky felt a twinge of jealousy watching the two of them in such a cozy setting. He turned away. Why did Scruggs have to show up and ruin everything? Just when he and Marta were starting to . . .

Forget it, he thought. And Shana, too. How could

she have taken up with Scruggs and his delinquent friends? How could the Weekender be going on right now with Shana back at Chautauqua and him stuck up here with his archenemy? It wasn't fair.

He couldn't resist looking back at Marta, whispering softly to Scruggs as she rocked him, stroking his shoulder.

Suddenly, Nicky couldn't care less what Shana did.

Chapter 10

Nicky awoke to daylight. Shaking the fuzziness from his head, he stared blankly at the rock ceiling. Where am I? he wondered. Gradually it came back to him, like a forgotten lie. The Weekender, getting lost, the snow, Marta. And now, Scruggs.

He knew, without looking, the fire was dead. So much for his plan to stay awake, keep the fire going, and play the part of caveman hero by protecting Marta—even though she hadn't shown any sign that she needed his protection.

The three had finally settled down under the meager blanket, owing their night's sleep more to exhaustion rather than comfort.

Nicky raised to one elbow and peered over Scruggs' still form at Marta, who was still asleep. Last evening it had crossed his mind that this was the first time in his life he'd spent an entire night with a girl. Somehow this wasn't exactly the way he thought it would be. First, he'd always pictured himself with a bashful, clinging girl, who looked to him for all the answers. Okay, so that was incredibly sexist, he told himself. But Martinella Lee Prigmore was as far from being a bashful, clinging girl as the three of them were from civilization. Yet he liked her just the way she was. So much for his stereotypical fantasies.

Second, in his dream of spending the night with a girl, he'd certainly never pictured Scruggs as part of the scene. A feeling of disgust rolled over him. Here was the person who annoyed him more than a pulled tendon before a track meet, sleeping in between him and Marta, just because of his condition. Nicky wished he could've slept a little closer to Marta last night. He felt the twinge again.

She shifted, coming awake, looking over Scruggs' head at Nicky. They smiled at each other while Scruggs snored.

"Gee, it's so romantic being here alone with you like this," Nicky joked.

Marta looked embarrassed. Sitting up, she shoved out from under the blanket, then tucked it around Scruggs' body. Glancing around, she hugged herself to keep warm. "Oh, no, the fire is out. And look!"

Nicky sat up to follow her gaze. A wall of snow was piled against the rocks and logs outside the shelter, leaving just enough space at the top for daylight to flood in and wake them. The huge drift had probably helped block the wind all night, Nicky decided, but now they'd have to dig their way out.

"I can't deal with anything until I get a fire going and eat first." Nicky came to his feet in slow motion, stretching his stiff, sore muscles. Checking the wood they'd brought in, he found it still as damp as it had been last night. The few pieces of leftover dry kindling and dead branches weren't enough to bother with. He caught Marta's eye. "Well, so much for a fire." The walls of the shelter were closing in on him, in addition to his being cold and hungry. "Let's just get out of here."

Marta had scooped snow into her gloved hand and was washing her face with it. Scruggs, now awake, sat

70

up to watch her. She smiled at him, catching her breath from the ice-cold snow. "How are you feeling?"

"Terrible."

She combed her hair with her fingers, foregoing the hat she'd loaned to Scruggs. "I don't know your name," she said, acting polite and friendly.

Scruggs grinned and held out a hand. "Sid Scruggman." He smirked at Nicky while Marta shook his hand, then he followed her movements with his eyes, a puzzled look on his face that didn't escape Nicky's observation.

No one's ever been so nice to him before, Nicky reasoned as he listened to Marta bring Scruggs up to date on their situation. He doesn't know how to react to undeserved kindness.

"We might as well eat breakfast before we start digging." Marta's morning voice squeaked more than usual as she tried to sound cheery. "How about scrambled lemon drops with hash brown lemon drops on the side and a cup of snow?"

"As if we had a choice," Nicky mumbled.

"I put the candy in the jacket you're wearing," she said to Scruggs as she reached into his pocket and pulled out an empty package.

Scruggs had a funny look on his face.

Nicky stared at the empty package. "You *ate* them? You ate *all* of them?" He didn't wait for an answer as he snatched the package from Marta, wadded it up, and threw it back at Scruggs. "How could you be so stupid? That was our only food!"

Scruggs cringed. "I—I didn't know that was our food supply. I was starving last night, and I didn't fall asleep as easily as you two. I found the candy in my pocket—so I ate it."

"It never occurred to you—"

71

"Nicky," Marta said in a low voice, taking hold of his jacket sleeve as if to stop him from injuring their already injured guest.

Scruggs ignored Nicky, bending close to Marta, one hand on her shoulder. "I'm sorry, Marta. *Believe me.*" His mock sincerity made Nicky want to throw up.

Mentally cursing at Scruggs with every swear word he'd ever heard since the day he was born, Nicky pushed away from Marta's grasp. He and Marta could have survived this ordeal fine, just the two of them. But now Scruggs had to come along and ruin everything.

Ripping off his gloves, Nicky clawed at the snowdrift blocking their escape. "Let's get out of here before I do something I won't be sorry for later."

Chapter 11

It took over an hour to clear away enough snow to get Scruggs out of the shelter. His leg was more swollen than it had been the night before, so he couldn't bend or lift it. Marta and Nicky had to drag him over the drifted snow at the mouth of the shelter.

Once outside, their spirits rose as the sun broke through the gray-muddled sky. Still, the snow was deep and the air was deathly cold. After a few false starts and much arguing, they finally agreed that the best arrangement for traveling was to put Scruggs in the middle, wearing the backpack, with one arm around each of the other two for balance.

Every few feet of movement brought a string of curses from Scruggs. Nicky wanted to stuff a handful of snow-covered rocks down his throat. The jerk's words didn't bother Nicky, but it didn't seem right for Marta to put up with Scruggs's profanity.

Nicky tried to speak low into Scruggs' left ear so Marta wouldn't hear, "Watch your mouth, or I'll—"

"Sid, I'd appreciate it if you wouldn't talk that way."

At first, Nicky didn't know who Sid was, then he remembered the name switch Scruggs had pulled on Marta. Scruggs immediately shut up at Marta's request, apologizing profusely. Terrific, Nicky thought, she won't even let me defend her honor.

Marta stopped the group by a small grove of trees, and dug through the snow until she found a semi-straight stick, about three feet long. She made Scruggs lean against a tree while she braced his leg with the stick, tying it on with strips of cloth she'd ripped from a T-shirt the bear had already shredded.

No one spoke as Marta worked, but her soft words and homemade splint did the trick to quiet Scruggs' complaining—better than Nicky's threats would have done.

As they started off again, Nicky raised his face to the sky, breathing in the freezing air. Clouds moved rapidly across the sun. The instant it was covered, the temperature seemed to drop ten degrees. Then the clouds would swirl away, allowing the sun to break through and warm Nicky's face. In a few seconds, the cycle would repeat itself. Warming and chilling. Warming and chilling.

He scanned the area as they hiked, looking for any sign familiar enough to jar his memory from yesterday. Everything appeared different in the bright, frosty daylight. The forest was breathtakingly beautiful, with branches of trees bowed low, heavy with snow. But the continuous white scenery had a sameness about it that made it easy to confuse directions. After only a few minutes of hiking, Nicky knew that without their footprints to follow, he'd never find his way back to the shelter.

As he moved, his photographer's eye caught the intricate detail of ice-laden twigs. Again, he wished he'd remembered his camera. At least watching for unusual angles of common objects released his mind from the worries at hand.

Nicky leaned around Scruggs to study Marta's profile. Unaware of his attention, she concentrated on keeping her balance as they hiked. He wished he could take pictures of her. Capture all her lively expressions forever on film. Maybe when they got home he could photograph her. It was something to look forward to, meaning he had to get off this endless mountain alive and go on with his life.

Traveling was slow and exasperating. Scruggs kept stopping to rest his leg, which made Nicky accuse him of doing the least work of all three of them. Marta was the referee. All the while, Nicky tried to ignore the hunger pains jabbing at his stomach. He vowed not to be the first to mention it.

Slipping for the umpteenth time, Nicky fell to one knee before he could catch himself. The other two stopped while he pulled himself up. They seemed to be taking turns getting off-balance since it was impossible to tell if they were stepping on a rock, log, flat ground, or even into a hidden stream with each step. No one said anything as Nicky got ready to move again. They'd stopped yelling at each other about it an hour ago.

Nearby, a wild animal howled. The closeness of the sudden, eerie noise startled them. Scruggs stopped.

"What are we stopping for now?" Nicky's stomach was in a knot. A hungry knot.

"Wolves! There are wolves around!"

"So what?" Nicky didn't think anything on earth would ever scare him as badly as the episode with the bear had.

Scruggs looked worried. "We should have some kind of a weapon to protect ourselves—don't you think?" He turned to Nicky.

"Don't ask me. Ask our personal encyclopedia on your right."

They both looked at Marta. "Well," she responded modestly. "I'm not sure wolves inhabit this part of the Rockies. It may be a coyote. But if there are wolves around, they already know we're here, and they're keeping their distance. Wolves are afraid of people."

Nicky had to admit he felt relieved.

"Besides," she continued. "Wolves only kill for food, and I don't think half-frozen teenagers are part of their diet."

Scruggs didn't look convinced. "But I saw this movie once about a pack of wolves who attacked a campground, killed all the adults, and kidnapped the children."

Nicky gave a short laugh.

"Yeah." Scruggs looked at him as if he'd just heard the story on the evening news.

"How'd the wolves kidnap the children?" Nicky asked in a mock serious tone. "With guns?"

Marta was laughing, too. "The story probably came out of some writer's imagination."

That seemed to satisfy Scruggs as they started off again. Nicky decided not to mention the bear. If Scruggs got this upset over a threat he couldn't even see, how would he have handled their confrontation with an animal who *would* eat half-frozen teenagers?

After a few minutes of silent struggling, Scruggs blurted, "What about snakes?"

"Snakes?" Marta and Nicky repeated together.

"Even *I* know the answer to that." Nicky tried not to gloat as he continued. "They're hibernating underground. Right, Marta?"

"Well, I don't know if it's called hibernation when you're referring to snakes, but you're right, they're

76

underground. Snakes come out to sun themselves on warm days in the winter, but I don't think we need to worry about that." Nicky noticed her grinning at Scruggs. "Are you really afraid of getting eaten by a snake?"

"No," Scruggs retorted. "*Bitten* by a snake—*eaten* by a wolf."

Marta laughed with him.

Nicky was beginning to feel left out. "Well, what about ticks? We could die of Rocky Mountain tick fever, too." He hoped Marta didn't think he was actually afraid of a measly bug, but he wanted to be included in their conversation.

"Tick season is long over," she answered. "Any other calamities you want to discuss?"

"How about buffalo stampedes, typhoid epidemics, and Indian raids?" offered Nicky.

"We're a hundred years too late to worry about those," she answered. "What else?"

"How about starvation and freezing to death?" Scruggs' voice had lost its playfulness.

For a few minutes no one spoke. Their moods had lightened with the jesting, and it seemed to make them move faster through the snowdrifts. Why did Scruggs have to bring them back to reality by mentioning things they couldn't avoid?

"Marta?" Scruggs' voice was so soft Nicky could barely hear him. "How come you know so much about all these things?"

"For every birthday I've had since I was eight, my grandfather has given me a book on wildlife, camping, or something like that."

"Well, Little Red Riding Hood," Scruggs whispered just loud enough so Nicky could hear, "I think you're incredible."

An awkward silence followed. Nicky wished someone would bring up a more interesting subject to discuss. He didn't want to spend the day watching a relationship grow between his worst enemy and the girl he was developing a mad crush on.

How could she be so nice to this creep? Nicky wondered. Especially after she'd let *him* hold her and kiss her last night. He thought she liked him. Maybe she was just being nice because he was the only guy around. Would Eve have married Adam if she'd had a choice? In anger, Nicky tried to move faster, throwing the other two off-balance. He didn't bother to apologize anymore.

Then he remembered that Marta was new at Mitchell High. She didn't know Scruggs or anything about him. She wasn't aware of his reputation around school, or the goons he hung out with. Nor did she know Scruggs was the reason Nicky'd been in such a bad mood at the beginning of the scavenger hunt.

Earlier, Marta had said she enjoyed being with him. *Him.* So maybe she did like him a little. Unless she went in for the body building type, like Scruggs, and had changed her mind.

Maybe he could get Marta alone and warn her about their third wheel. He wanted terribly to hold her again and tell her how special she was—before Scruggs beat him to it. If only they could be alone for a little while.

Nicky surveyed the unchanging whiteness surrounding them. Fat chance, he thought.

Chapter 12

By afternoon the elusive sun had disappeared for the last time behind dark clouds. A frigid wind kicked up, whirling giant snowflakes around the weary group. Their spirits couldn't have been lower at the prospect of spending another cold night in the wilderness. Wasn't anyone out there looking for them? Nicky wondered. Had they been walking in circles all day?

He'd read stories in the newspaper about rescue parties searching for stranded skiers, travelers, or plane crash victims in the mountains. Shivering, he recalled one story about a plane which crashed in the high country in a valley unreachable by search parties during the winter months. The bodies of the victims weren't discovered until the snow melted late in the spring.

Nicky felt more sympathy for the poor soul who stumbled across the partially decomposed bodies than he did for the dead people. What a heart-stopper that would be.

He forced from his mind the image of someone stumbling across the three of them in six or seven months. He could visualize the newspaper account: "Missing teens found at last. It appears that two of them, long time adversaries, murdered each other. The third one apparently died from knowing all the answers."

Nicky chuckled in spite of himself. But the fear of not getting home today made him want to cry. He doubted they'd be lucky enough to find a shelter as handy as the one they'd slept in last night. And even if they did, there was still no food.

He felt as if he'd run two marathons back to back after not eating for a week. The others were showing signs of weakness, too, but he admitted that Scruggs was worse off than he or Marta because of his injury. He'd tried to put on his almost-dry jeans, but they no longer fit. He had to leave Marta's warm-ups on, which were tight on his bad leg.

Marta had whispered something to Nicky about frostbite, but if Scruggs was in fact suffering from frostbite, it had happened before they'd rescued him, and there wasn't a whole lot they could do about it now. He definitely needed medical attention. The sooner, the better.

They stopped to rest, sitting in the snow because there was nowhere else to sit. Nicky turned his back on the others. He found the attention Scruggs was giving Marta annoying. Why did she have to be so friendly to him? And why did Scruggs have to travel in the middle so Nicky couldn't talk to her without the jerk listening?

After a few minutes of trying not to eavesdrop on their conversation, Nicky's exasperation got the better of him. "I think we should quit avoiding the topic of food," he blurted, interrupting them. He hated breaking his vow about not being the first to mention his hunger, but he was feeling weak and dizzy, even nauseous. And Scruggs seemed to be having greater difficulty dragging his bad leg. Except for the bag of lemon drops, he'd had less food than they.

80

Marta had gotten too quiet the last few hours. Her freckles seemed to stand out darker than normal against her pale face.

Nicky went on. "I know it's possible to survive without food longer than water—and water's no problem with all this snow. But how much longer can we travel without food for energy?"

Scruggs fell backward into a drift. "This is it for me," he said, groaning. "I can't take another step."

Marta was quiet for a moment. "You guys are talking yourself into defeat." She rose to lean against a tree trunk, looking rather defeated herself. "Your mind can work for you or against you. If you focus on how much your body hurts and how hungry you are, you'll convince your brain that you can't go on—and your body will obey. If that's the case, we might as well give up right now and never leave this spot. We can stay right here forever, feeding the animals, so to speak."

Nicky tried to ignore her last comment as he leaned forward to listen. He was now fascinated with the squeaky voice that earlier had scraped on his nerves.

"The trick is to focus outside yourself," Marta continued, her voice picking up enthusiasm with each word. "Picture Camp Chautauqua, because that's where we're headed. Your pain and hunger will still be there, but you won't notice it as much." She paused while her audience groaned in unison.

"All right, I know I'm not the one with the injury, but I'm just as cold and hungry as you guys. And you both weigh a lot more than I do. I'd be the first to die."

Marta brushed windblown hair from her face. "I feel funny telling you this, but when I'm hiking alone, I sing to myself. It forces me to concentrate on the song and not on myself, how sore my legs are, or whether or not I'm getting blisters.'' She looked embarrassed, as if she expected them to laugh at her. ''It's a trick my grandfather taught me. Singing makes time go by faster, too. Try it.''

Marta returned Nicky's gaze as if she were really concerned that every muscle in his body had gone on strike.

''You're crazy,'' he said in a soft voice. ''You have it all worked out, don't you? A system for everything you do. And now you've discovered a painless way to die.''

Nicky rose and kissed her on the cheek, not caring whether or not Scruggs was watching. ''If we ever get home, promise you'll teach me how to organize my life as well as yours?''

''I know ridicule when I hear it.'' She flipped a handful of snow into his face. ''Okay, *be* in pain. See if I try to help you again.'' As she reached to wipe the snow from his cheek, he caught her gloved hand and squeezed it.

''Getting back to the main problem,'' Scruggs began, cutting off Nicky and Marta's playfulness. He acted as if their flirtatiousness bothered him the same way it bothered Nicky when the tables were turned. ''I always thought when people were lost in a forest, they survived by eating nuts and berries.''

''Yeah.'' Nicky hated agreeing with Scruggs, but the same thought had crossed his mind. He turned to Marta. ''You're the one who was reading *Tips on Backpacking and How to Survive*. What did it say about food?''

She looked a bit sheepish. ''Would you believe I hadn't gotten to that chapter yet?''

Nicky loved catching her unprepared, throwing a

topic at her she didn't know anything about, even though her lack of knowledge might prove fatal.

"*However*," she continued, unwilling to give up. "From what I've read in other books, we have to be careful not to eat anything that happens to be poison."

"Makes sense," Scruggs replied. "How can we tell?"

"We're supposed to watch the animals, then eat what they eat, and avoid what they avoid." Marta moved around for warmth. Snow was falling heavier now, and lack of movement was enough to let the chill creep in. "Of course we're not going to find any animals in the middle of a storm, so that's not going to work." She glanced at Nicky. "We saw a lot of wildlife yesterday, but none today. That's not a good sign. Animals can sense an impending storm. They're smart enough to take shelter when the weather turns dangerous."

Scruggs chuckled. "I saw a lot of wildlife yesterday myself—but no animals." He laughed at his own pun, then sobered when the other two didn't respond. "So, what you're saying is, if the wolves and poison berries don't get us, we'll merely freeze to death."

"You need to practice Marta's method of mind over matter." Nicky was feeling much less hostile toward the new side his old enemy was showing him—a vulnerable, fearful side.

Nicky studied his profile. It surprised him that Scruggs seemed overly concerned about dying—not that Nicky wasn't, but he preferred to keep his worries inside and not voice them. Scruggs always came across like nothing ever bothered him, much less the hazards of the wilderness.

Truth sifted into Nicky's mind like the neverending

snowflakes. Scruggs, stripped of his bodyguards, was nothing more than a coward.

"Let's get going, guys," Marta said, squinting at the uncooperative sky. "I hope someone comes up with a brilliant plan for dinner soon. Maybe we'll stumble across a McDonald's over the next hill. Who knows?"

They started out again, moving even slower. Nicky was trying to be more tolerant of Scruggs after his sudden burst of insight about his long-time enemy. But it was difficult. He still resented Scruggs for coming between him and Marta.

After a while they came to a stream, flowing clear below a thin layer of ice. Nicky hesitated. "I think I can chip through to the fresh water underneath and fill up the plastic bottle." He knelt on the bank, pulled off a glove, and knocked on the ice with his knuckles to test its thickness. "Scruggs, get the bottle and iodine tablets out of the pack."

"I've trained you well," teased Marta. "I'll make a mountain man out of you yet." She stopped to scrutinize their surroundings. "While you're doing that, I'm hiking over yonder hill to find the Ladies' Room, if you know what I mean."

"And I'm headed for the opposite hill," Scruggs said after tossing the bottle and tablets to Nicky. "That's where the Men's Room is."

They all laughed together for the first time. Nicky watched Scruggs hobble away, feeling guilty for not offering to help him up the rise. "Be careful," Nicky called, meaning it for Marta, but addressing it to both of them.

After they disappeared, he turned his attention to the stream. Scooping snow out of the way, he chipped at the ice with the handle of the flashlight, wondering if this could be the same stream he and Marta had picnicked at yesterday. Had it been only yesterday?

A few moments later, Nicky heard the ice beside him crack. Startled, he swiveled on his knees, coming face to face with a playful black bear cub.

Nicky leaped to his feet, alarmed. The cub scampered across the ice and up a steep hill on the other side of the stream. As Nicky started to turn, a deep growl raised the hair on the back of his neck. The next second, he was slammed to the ground. His head hit the ice and everything went blank.

Chapter 13

As Nicky's consciousness slowly returned, he saw a light at the end of a black whirling funnel. In the light, Marta's face appeared. Her lips were moving but there was no sound. Her face shimmered, the features shifting until it became Shana's face. Then the light burst through the funnel and he saw nothing but snow and more snow, as Scruggs's sneering voice shouted, "Nicholas!" over and over.

Slowly the fog in his brain cleared until he could open his eyes. Marta was wiping blood from his face with the corner of her jacket, and kissing him. Her lips were wet and salty. "Nicky?" she sobbed. "Please be okay. Scruggs is hurt badly."

"Scruggs?" The name came out more of a moan than a word. "How . . . ?" Nicky was confused.

"He was on his way back from the top of the hill when he saw the bear. He ran as fast as he could with his bad leg, and threw himself on top of you. You fell and hit your head on the ice, then the bear attacked him."

Marta paused to wipe her eyes on her sleeve. "The bear was just protecting her cub. Scruggs must have scared them. She knocked him down and scratched him—maybe even bit him—I don't know. His head hit a rock when he fell and he's unconscious."

Nicky pulled himself up and leaned on one elbow. The scenery around him was spinning. Scruggs sprawled in the snow next to the stream. His clothes were ripped and blood was everywhere, melting the snow with its warmth.

Marta sat back on her knees, crying. "I'd just come over the hill and I saw the whole thing. It was horrible. What would I do if both of you were unconscious?" She tried to stop crying as if she were telling herself she could handle it. "We've got to save him, Nicky. He saved your life."

Nicky crawled toward Scruggs to assess his condition. Marta helped him pull off Scruggs' jacket, peel up the sweater, and open his shirt to determine how severe his injuries were. Nicky couldn't find any deep puncture wounds to indicate the bear had actually bitten him, just some mean-looking scratches in spite of the heavy layers of clothing. He didn't know how severe they were, but if they were bad enough to bleed, they were bad enough to get infected.

Nicky helped Marta clean the wounds with handfuls of snow. They wrapped pieces of Scruggs' flannel shirt around those still bleeding slightly, then bundled him up as warmly as they could. A bloody bump was forming on Scruggs' forehead. They cleaned it, but had nothing to cover it with.

Nicky stood with rubbery knees and pulled Marta to her feet. He put his fingers to his head, which was still spinning. The bleeding from his wound had stopped, telling him the dizziness must be from lack of food, not loss of blood.

Marta watched his face, tears sliding down her cheeks. He pulled her close, kissed her, and wiped away her tears with his gloved hand. An unexpected feeling of happiness washed over him. He'd survived a night in a storm, a bear attack, almost starving to death, and now he had Marta's undivided attention again. And she was actually crying and acting as if *she* needed *him*.

"Don't worry," he told her. "We saved him once; we'll do it again. Everything will be all right." He held her while she cried. It felt so good to hold her, to feel her clutching him tightly. Watching the bear attack must have been more terrible than being in the middle of it. He never knew what hit him—never even saw the bear, only the cub.

"Are you okay?" He wasn't in any hurry to let go of her, but he felt guilty leaving Scruggs lying unattended in the snow. "We'll have to carry Scruggs out of here. Do you think you can do it?"

Marta pulled back, sniffling and wiping her eyes with her jacket sleeve. "I read a book once on wilderness rescues, and it said—"

Nicky put a finger to her lips and whispered, "No more lectures, Ms. Encyclopedia. We'll figure something out—together."

He couldn't read the look on her face but he hoped she was pleased with the way he was taking charge, considering his injury.

"Okay," she agreed, lifting her chin to meet his gaze, transforming into the old Martinella right before his eyes.

"That's my girl," he whispered. His words surprised him almost as much as they must have surprised her. Reluctantly, he let go of her.

Marta stood motionless while Nicky prepared to leave. It was up to him to carry the pack now, as well as carry Scruggs. The pack was almost empty, and he was tempted to leave it behind. But the material or the frame might come in handy later. Besides, the pack wasn't his to throw away. It was Marta's birthday present.

Sighing with weariness, Nicky wondered how he was supposed to carry someone who weighed more than he did. He'd just have to focus outward, and not think about his own aches and pains and hunger, as Marta had suggested.

"Ready?" He circled Scruggs' prone body, trying to figure a way to lift him without causing further injury. "If you walk in front and hold Scruggs' legs, I'll have the bulk of his weight against me, and—"

"No."

He looked at her grim face.

"What's the matter?"

She hesitated, twisting a loose curl through her gloved fingers. "We have to stay here."

"What?" Nicky wondered if she'd gotten too upset to be rational.

"We can't keep traveling."

"Marta, Scruggs needs a doctor." In the still forest Nicky's voice sounded loud as it rose in volume. "He needs a *hospital!* We've got to get him out of here." Nicky felt panic flood over him at the reality of his own words. "We've got to get *us* out of here."

"Nicky, listen." Marta kept her voice low, but her fingers tugged harder at the curl. "I know you think I'm crazy, and I may be taking a chance, but when we were cleaning Scruggs' wounds, didn't you wonder why he wasn't bleeding heavier?"

Nicky glanced around at the blood-stained snow and shook his head. "I thought it was good that he wasn't gushing blood. What would we have done then?"

"Made a tourniquet to stop the flow," she answered without missing a beat. "But *lack* of heavy bleeding means he's in shock." She sank to her knees beside

Scruggs. "I checked for other signs, just to be sure."
She grabbed Nicky's hand and pulled him next to her.
"Here, feel his pulse."

He let Marta guide his fingers to a spot under
Scruggs' chin. His pulse was beating fast and hard.

"And feel his skin."

Nicky followed her lead, not really wanting to touch
Scruggs. His skin was cold and damp.

"Nicky, he's in shock; I know he is. We'll have to
keep him warm and still."

Nicky paused. He'd convinced himself they were
only around the corner from Chautauqua. But if they
stopped and stayed here, their chances of getting back
before they starved to death weren't so good. He
remembered the story of the girl who died only ten feet
from her house. Wouldn't it be ironic if Chautauqua
were over the next hill and they all died this close to
safety?

Marta looked as if she were ready to put up a fight
if he said no. "We could *kill* Scruggs if we tried to
carry him out of here. Especially the way we've been
stumbling through the deep snow just trying to walk."
The eyes that had the power to unnerve him pleaded
with his. "Scruggs' injuries aren't as serious as they
might have been. He's not going to die from them. But
he *could* die from shock. Is that a chance you're
willing to take?"

Nicky watched her face as she talked, believing
every word, but wishing she hadn't put the decision
upon his shoulders.

"Marta, we're in the middle of nowhere. There
aren't even any rocks around here for a shelter."

"Then we'll build one."

"Where?"

"Right here. No, wait." She squinted at the area

around them, then pointed to a grove of trees. "Right there. Between those two tallest trees. The snow there isn't as deep because of the overhanging branches. And look," she added, holding out her hand. "The snow has stopped and the sun's trying to come out. Maybe it will melt what's under our feet and we'll find out we're standing right on top of a trail."

Nicky couldn't believe her undying enthusiasm, or how she made him feel as though they were merely playing a game. He gazed at the sun's feeble attempt to shine through the gloom, still not convinced. "We build a shelter, and then what? Stay here and starve to death?"

Marta was acting impatient. She plowed her way to the grove of trees to survey the area. "My grandfather always said that it's better to do *something*, even if it's *wrong*, than to do nothing at all. I'm just following my instincts, and my instincts are telling me to stay here until it's safe to move Scruggs."

Nicky watched her struggle back to him, apparently satisfied with the spot she'd chosen. "What else did your grandfather always say?" he asked in a flat voice.

"Always prepare for the worst, then hope for the best."

Nicky hadn't expected her to answer so quickly. She wedged the backpack under Scruggs' feet to elevate them, explaining that it would allow blood to flow back to the heart more easily. Then she took the knife from her pocket and began cutting evergreen boughs from the lower branches of a nearby tree.

Nicky trudged toward her, stepping in her foot imprints, too tired to plow his own way through the fresh layer. "I'll do that. You keep an eye on Scruggs."

She ignored his order, taking one of the boughs back

to the grove, using it as a broom to sweep snow from between the two tall trees.

He watched her struggle with the weight of the heavy, wet snow. His arms were tiring fast, too, as he twisted and cut at the evergreen boughs. He kept one eye on Scruggs as he worked, because he thought he'd heard him moan once.

After Marta had finished clearing a small area, Nicky placed branches down to pad the ground. Carefully, they lifted Scruggs and carried him to the boughs, elevating his feet again, then wrapping the worn blanket tightly around his still frame.

Nicky helped Marta scout logs for a lean-to. One was used as a ridgepole to connect the trees. They placed it on top of two thick branches about five feet off the ground. The other logs sloped from the ridge-pole to the ground, creating a semicircle around Scruggs.

At Marta's command, Nicky collected a few small saplings that had already fallen from the weight of the snow. Awkwardly, he helped her weave the saplings between the thin logs at an angle to make a quilt-like pattern, being careful not to step on Scruggs' feet sticking out of the entrance.

Nicky sharpened the saplings at one end with the knife, then did his best to drive the slanted ends into the ground, which wasn't frozen too deeply yet since it was only October.

He became so intent on building the lean-to that at first he didn't notice the droning sound that started as quietly as a bee hum, then exploded into his mind with a roar.

"A helicopter!" he shouted, running from the grove into the open area by the stream. He jumped up and down with whatever energy he had left, waving his arms. Marta stayed behind, fumbling wildly through the pack.

"Hurry!" Nicky yelled at her. He felt as if he wanted to laugh and cry at the same time. They were being rescued! Frantically, he tried to think of other ways to attract attention. "A mirror!" he yelled at her. "Bring me your mirror so we can signal!"

Marta stumbled into the open area just as the helicopter came into view. She thrust a torn, crumpled piece of aluminum foil at him.

"What's this for?" he shouted.

"Signal with it!"

There wasn't time to argue, so Nicky tried desperately to bounce the reflection of the half-hidden sun off the measly piece of foil, while Marta danced around in the snow, waving one hand wildly and holding up a piece of her broken glasses with the other, trying to catch the dim light from the sun.

In a few seconds the helicopter was gone, as quickly as it had appeared. They both stood stone-still, the quiet droning sound teasing their ears, their brief spurt of energy draining away.

Nicky whipped around to face Marta. "Why didn't you bring me a mirror like I asked? They would have seen us then!"

"I don't have a mirror!"

"All girls have mirrors!"

"I'm not . . . all girls. . . ." Marta's voice broke in a high-pitched squeak. "I'm just me and I don't have a mirror." She bit her lower lip and turned away.

Nicky felt exhausted, more from the disappointment than anything else. They'd come so close. As he looked at Marta, his heart turned over inside his chest. For someone so small and helpless looking, she certainly wasn't. Yet, when she cried, it made him feel strong. It gave him a chance to help her for a change, even though he felt like crying, too. What did they have to look forward to now?

Nicky held out his arms and she collapsed into them, giving in to the tears. They rocked back and forth, crying together and holding on to each other as the short-lived afternoon sun disappeared for the last time behind a mountain peak. Nicky's emotions seemed as fickle as the sunshine. He wondered why he couldn't control them around Marta.

"Do you think they saw us?" Her voice was muffled.

"I don't know." he whispered. Her hair smelled like wood smoke from last night's fire. "If they saw us, they'll probably circle around and come back again." He knew there hadn't been enough sunlight to make the reflectors work, but he didn't say it.

Nicky wasn't sure how long they stood there, wrapped in each other's arms, ears alert, straining to hear the faint hum of the returning helicopter.

It never came.

Chapter 14

Marta completed the lean-to by overlapping pine boughs down the sides. She secured them by twisting and intertwining the branches together with those of the saplings. Nicky helped as best he could with frozen fingers, trying to ignore his growing uneasiness about Scruggs. He'd assumed Scruggs would snap out of it by now, and revert to his offensive personality for no other reason than to spite Nicky. Occasionally, Scruggs moaned, but he didn't move or open his eyes.

After Nicky fashioned a makeshift door for the lean-to out of pine boughs, they worked in silence preparing a place for a fire outside the door opening. They didn't have to erect an umbrella this time, since the snow had stopped falling, but they did pile logs behind the fire to serve as a heat reflector since it had worked well the night before.

Nicky gathered dead branches that were kept dry on the trees by the canopy of branches over them. He combined these with some kindling and small logs Marta had salvaged from the shelter and stashed in the pack.

He managed to get a flame going, using the matches sealed in fingernail polish. As their match supply dwindled, each one became as precious as food. Finally, they could relax next to the fire with the shelter of the lean-to surrounding them. It was almost cozy.

Nicky pulled Marta onto his lap, facing the fire, and wrapped his arms around her knees. "I'm sorry I yelled at you earlier." His cheek rested against her ear.

"I'm not sorry I yelled back."

He drew away, surprised. "You're not? Oh yeah," he teased. "Redheads are supposed to have fiery temperaments."

"That's not what I meant. I think we both felt better after we yelled at each other." She glanced back at him. "All day I've felt the tension building between us—the three of us, I mean. Yelling at the top of my lungs made me feel a lot better."

"I guess you're right." Nicky pretended to hold a microphone to his mouth. "Well, folks, not only does she talk like an encyclopedia, she can also sound like a walking psychology textbook. What next?" He held the invisible microphone in front of her.

Marta laughed, pushing his hand away. "I've still got work to do," she said, giving a heavy sigh.

"What's there to do? We've done all we can for Scruggs. Let's relax a while. Maybe go out to a movie later, then get a PIZZA!" His yell echoed through the darkening trees.

"There are still things we can do. Things we should have done already."

"For instance?"

"For instance, we should be making plans to stay right where we are. Why did we bawl Scruggs out for not staying where Shana left him when we've been moving constantly, not knowing if we're hiking toward Chautauqua, further away, or around in circles?"

"You mean we should have stayed on the cliff when we first realized we were lost?"

"Probably. Or nearby—at the rock shelter."

"That's funny. Back in elementary school they taught us to find a tree the minute we realized we were lost, sit under it, and stay there until we were found." Nicky chuckled. "I guess I thought I was too old to follow such a simple rule."

"That's why so many people get lost in the mountains. They underestimate the dangers of the wilderness."

Nicky hugged her to him. "Okay, I've learned my lesson. Can I go home now?"

She ignored his question. "I need your help. We should set up distress signals. If we'd done it by now, the helicopter pilot would have seen them from the air, and we'd probably be home by now. We should set them up before it gets dark, in case the copter comes back."

Nicky knew it was too late in the evening for the helicopter to return, but he didn't mention it. There was always tomorrow. He *hoped* there'd be a tomorrow. "What are the signals?"

"Well, I didn't memorize them." Marta closed her eyes, trying to think. "I can only remember two. Logs laid in the shape of an *F* mean we need food." She thought some more, pulling Nicky's arms tighter around her for warmth. "The only other shape I can remember is an *X*, which means we're stranded and can't move on."

"Those two are the only signals we need." He hated to get up, more because he'd have to release his hold on Marta than for any other reason. "Let's do it now; it won't take long."

Marta pulled herself up and he followed, stretching. They chose seven medium-sized logs, already fallen, and dragged them to the clearing by the stream. Nicky arranged four of them in a giant *X*, and Marta arranged the other three into an *F*. Nicky sat on one of the logs to rest while Marta dusted snow off the tops. The signals would be useless if they were covered with snow, blending in with the rest of the whiteness.

"Are you saying we should stay here even if Scruggs regains consciousness and can move again?"

"Yes. That's what my instincts are telling me now."

"We'll starve to death." Nicky stood and helped her dust off the snow so they could get back to the warmth of the fire. "Look at us, Marta. We have no energy, and we're yelling at each other."

"Ha," she answered. "If you remember correctly, Mr. Brooks, we were yelling at each other long before we got lost, much less hungry."

Nicky had to agree.

"Besides the distress signals, we should have been looking for food all along. It was stupid not to. I was so sure we'd find our way back to camp, that I didn't want to waste time collecting food."

Nicky took her gloved hand as they walked back to the lean-to. Their many trips had created a pathway through the snow, so it wasn't such an effort to walk now. "I thought we'd make it back to Chautauqua today, too, or they'd find us." He paused. "Who was it that said 'Prepare for the worst, then hope for the best'?"

She acted surprised that he remembered. "My grandfather. I guess we did one but not the other." She threw a gaze upward. "Sorry, Grandpa."

Nicky followed her gaze. "Is he . . . ?"

"Yeah, he died a few months ago, which is the reason I moved to Colorado."

Nicky didn't get the connection.

"He and my dad were partners in a mountaineering

supply business which had to be sold after Grandpa died. Moving out here was my dad's fresh start.''

Marta's voice dropped to a whisper as she talked about her grandfather. Nicky wished he could say something to make her feel better.

"It's going to be hard on my dad to lose another member of his family so quickly, but—'' Stopping abruptly, she hurried ahead to the sputtering fire and poked at it with a nearby stick.

At first Nicky didn't understand what she was implying. "Wait a minute. What do you mean? Lose another member of his family? Where's the old spunk, Martinella Lee Prigmore? Where's the old mind over matter programming?''

She didn't respond. Didn't even lift her head to look at him. He grabbed her sleeve to make her listen. "We didn't get rescued today, so what? Our distress signals are in place, we're going out for food now, and we'll have a dry, semi-warm place to sleep. What's the problem?''

She lifted her eyes to him. Dark circles he hadn't noticed before half-mooned under her eyes in the dimming light. She jerked away from him.

"Marta, what—?''

"Leave me alone.''

He reached for her again, but she twisted away from him and slipped into the lean-to. A few moments later she emerged with the empty water bottle. Nicky didn't know how to react to her abrupt mood change because he didn't know what was wrong.

He started to follow her into the trees, but she whipped around and faced him. "Alone!'' she yelled again.

Nicky retreated like a hurt puppy, knelt by the fire, and watched her go.

99

Chapter 15

As Nicky watched from a distance, Marta wedged the plastic bottle in the snow at the foot of a tree. Pulling a knife from her pocket, she carved a notch in the trunk above the bottle.

Nicky was confused—both about why she was carving on the tree, and why she was upset. He was the one with the mood swings, not Marta. He was always the first to yell. What had gotten into her?

In a few moments she trudged back to the lean-to, gave Nicky an apologetic look, then collapsed next to him by the fire.

"I'm sorry," she began.

"It's okay. People get grouchy when they're hungry."

"It's not that, Nicky, I need to talk to you about—"

"I said, it's okay. You're forgiven. Now, what were you doing to that poor, defenseless tree out there?"

She was quiet for a moment, as if trying to decide whether or not to pursue her explanation, then gave up with a sigh. "I tapped into the tree's sap supply. Enough should drip out during the course of the night to give us a few swallows in the morning."

"Plain tree sap?"

"It's nourishing. Once a man lived on nothing but

sweet sap for three weeks when his plane crashed in the Yukon.''

"I'd rather pour it as syrup over a plate of steaming pancakes with butter. Maybe add some strawberries and whipped cream on top for good measure.''

"You're only making it worse.''

Nicky glanced at the darkening sky. "Hey, if we're going to search for food before dark, we'd better get a move on.''

Marta rose. "Wait, I need to get the flashlight and check on Scruggs.'' In a minute, she climbed outside, shaking her head.

"Same?'' he asked.

"Same.'' She met his eyes, then looked away. "Come on, let's go hunt for our dinner. And bring your bow and arrow. Maybe we can shoot a tuna and make sandwiches to eat.''

Nicky followed her deeper into the grove, now breaking new snow. His legs rebelled, so he trained his thoughts on dinner instead. "What exactly are we looking for besides tuna? A pizza tree next to a Coke bush?''

"No. Leaves.''

"Leaves? You want me to eat *leaves?*''

"It's either that or insects.''

"I'll take the leaves.''

"Good choice, since all the insects have probably disappeared by now. If we get real desperate, I can set a snare for small animals, using a few twigs and my shoelaces.'' She studied her hiking boots with laces charred from holding the umbrella over last night's fire. She'd had to tie them together in knots. "Well, maybe with *your* shoelaces.''

Nicky stopped at a bush, shook the snow off the leaves, and held out the branch. "We have leaves. Are these edible or poisonous?'' He now felt comfortable relying on Marta's decisions.

She leaned over to study them. "They're okay. Fill your pockets, and I'll look near the stream. Lucky for us it's only October and all the leaves haven't fallen yet.'' She squinted at the evening sky. "Pick all you can find while we still have some light. We'll sort them later."

They returned to the lean-to when it became too dark to see. After they dumped their collection of plants, leaves, and roots onto a corner of the blanket, Nicky got the fire going again while Marta checked once more on Scruggs.

It was the first time all three of them had been inside the lean-to at the same time, and was a lot more cramped than the shelter had been.

As Nicky watched Marta sort leaves, his stomach rumbled at the prospect of eating something—anything. "Tell me what each pile is first," he said, feeling cautious about eating ordinary plants and remembering Scruggs' earlier worry about being poisoned.

"I don't know what each plant is," Marta admitted, "but just to be safe, don't eat anything that tastes bitter." She turned on the flashlight so she could see better. Nicky wondered how long the batteries would last and wished Marta would conserve them. His thinking had changed from "We'll be home in a matter of hours" to "What else can we do to ensure our survival?"

"These plants from beside the stream are bulrushes. They're okay. And those," Marta said, pointing to another pile, "are chicory leaves. They're okay." She looked up at Nicky. "I'm not sure what the others are, sorry." She gave a flourish with her arm. "Dinner is served. First course, a nature salad."

102

Nicky decided to be brave. He scooped a handful of chicory leaves and chewed them slowly, trying to choke as inconspicuously as he could. "Pass the water, please."

"Sorry, there isn't any. The bottle is busy collecting sap, remember?"

Nicky ignored his thirst and gulped the scratchy leaves. As he ate, the sharpness of his hunger diminished. At least he didn't feel as if he were on the verge of starving to death anymore.

Marta picked at the leaves, eating only a few. Nicky urged her to eat more, but she refused with no explanation. He was puzzled. She had to be as hungry as he was, but he didn't want to pursue the issue for fear she'd get upset at him again.

Maybe tomorrow they could actually catch a small rabbit or squirrel. Better yet, maybe they'd be home tomorrow.

As darkness fell, it became bitterly cold. Nicky built up the fire one last time, then reluctantly agreed that Scruggs should sleep in the middle again, even though he'd have preferred sleeping closer to Marta.

Nicky adjusted the blanket around the three of them. He hadn't realized how tired he was until he lay down, but at least he was spared from hunger tonight.

He watched the fire's reflection dance across the back of the lean-to as he listened to Scruggs' ragged breathing. "Do you think anyone's looking for us?" His voice bounced off the curved wall.

"Of course they are. Why do you think the Forest Service has Search and Rescue Teams? And they're busy all year round, not just in the winter."

"They probably rescue a lot of people from New Jersey who've never been in *real* mountains before."

Marta reached over Scruggs' still form and punched

Nicky in the side. "I've been in the mountains more times than you have."

After a long moment of silence, Marta's squeaky voice broke into his half-dream. "Nicky? Tomorrow is Monday. The Weekender is over, and everyone will be back at school. Except us."

How could it be only Monday? he thought, moaning a reply to Marta. It seemed as if they'd been lost for weeks.

He tried to turn over without losing his share of the blanket. Despite the extent of his tiredness, he couldn't fall asleep. His ears kept deceiving him with noises of animals and airplanes. His mind filled with images of the Weekender, his family, Marta.

"Marta?" he whispered even though he knew she was sleeping. "I really care about you. A lot."

The mysterious sounds of the night were his only answer.

Chapter 16

Nicky was the first one awake in the morning. He'd barely slept. The cold penetrated to a depth he didn't know was possible. Cold as death, his mind kept saying.

Staring at the roof of the lean-to, he thought back to Friday morning, and how he'd rushed to pack his clothes for the Weekender before it was time to leave for school.

His mom had thrown a load of laundry into the dryer on her way out the door for work, leaving him a note that said she'd washed his heavy wool socks and gloves.

Nicky had stopped the dryer to haul out his socks, then sprawled on the laundry room floor to pull them on. They were so warm, almost unbearably hot. He remembered fantasizing at the time what a luxury it would be to dress in pre-heated socks every winter day.

Now, as he wiggled his half-frozen toes inside his hiking boots, he was unable to imagine ever having warm feet again. Funny how he always rushed through life so fast, he never stopped to savor small luxuries like heated socks, chocolate chip cookies warm from the oven, a hot shower on a cold day. Pizza.

The thoughts warmed his mind but nothing else. He

longed for Marta's warmth, yet he hardly felt like snuggling up to Scruggs.

Nicky raised to one elbow. Scruggs looked terrible in the hazy light of early dawn. His skin seemed grayish, and the bones in his face jutted more prominently now. The bump on his forehead and the bruises on his cheek and chin from being knocked to the ground had turned a sickly, purplish-green color.

For one heart-stopping moment, Nicky thought Scruggs was dead. Then he saw the blanket across Scruggs' chest rise slightly with the intake of breath. He sighed with relief.

Nicky's eyes traveled to Marta, whose face seemed whiter than the narrow strip of sky he could see above the trees outside the lean-to. Her hair was becoming matted. She must have given up trying to comb it with her fingers. He'd never met a girl who didn't carry a comb or a mirror—they seemed to be standard equipment for girls at school.

I probably don't look so great myself, he thought, rubbing his smooth chin. He noticed with envy that Scruggs' chin was covered with dark whiskers.

The lean-to began closing in on him, so he crawled outside to stretch his legs. Standing straight, he jogged in place for a few minutes to warm himself, missing his morning runs. Every muscle in his body ached from sleeping on the damp, hard ground. "I feel like I'm a hundred years old," he grumbled as he headed toward the water bottle. Retrieving it, he brushed snow off a nearby rock for a place to sit.

It was then he noticed dark clouds rolling low across the sky, almost like thunderheads. A new snowflake tingled against his cheek. Terrific, he thought. Another storm. That's all they needed now. Searches were called off during bad weather. There'd be no helicopters sighting their distress signals if the storm was coming this way. Not only was it too dangerous to fly, but ground visibility would be zero.

Nicky tilted the bottle, letting a small amount of cold, thick sap flow around his finger. Licking it off, he scooped more. Sap didn't taste as bad as he thought it would. He repositioned the bottle under the notch in the tree, afraid to take too much. Maybe they could give the rest to Scruggs to help him regain his strength.

Nicky craved a hot, soapy shower and remembered he hadn't combed his hair for three days. Finding a long-forgotten comb wedged in his back pocket, he made a half-hearted attempt to untangle his hair. He didn't really care what he looked like; he had more important things to worry about.

Scooping snow into his cupped hands, he washed his face. It was more breathtaking than diving into the pond at his grandparents' house the spring he turned eleven—something else he hadn't thought about in years. Why was he remembering all these moments from his past? Did it mean he was going to die? The memory of his grandparents' pond twinged his heart with homesickness. After a couple more swipes with the icy handful of snow, Nicky decided staying dirty was preferable to freezing.

Marta stuck her head out of the lean-to. "Oh, no!" she exclaimed, taking in the clouds and new snowfall. Her eyes met Nicky's as she trudged their new pathway to join him on the flat rock.

She sat close, probably for warmth, he reminded himself. He felt sure that after her frustration with him last night she didn't like him any more. He brushed a few frizzy curls off her forehead.

"Don't move," Nicky ordered. He went after the bottle of sap and brought it back to her. "Breakfast is served," he said, handing over the bottle. "And, I have a surprise for you." Reaching into his pocket, he produced the comb. "Look what I found. No more finger combing."

She tasted the sap, then reached for the comb.

"No, let me." He drew her hair from under her jacket collar. "Meester Nick veel make you look mahvelous."

Finally she smiled, giving him a feeling as good as if the sun had burst through the gray clouds, making wildflowers shoot up through the snowdrifts and bloom.

After a few yanks and yells, Marta instructed him to begin at the bottom of her hair, working upward to smooth out the tangles. So what did he know about combing long hair? He watched her dip into the sap as he had earlier, licking it off her fingers.

"Take more," he urged, concerned at how frail she appeared this morning. Her clothes seemed to hang on her thin frame. "We can leave the bottle under the tree all day. You need the nourishment."

Hesitating, she took one more small scoop, then set the bottle aside. Nicky handed it back to her. "Marta, you need—"

"No." She gave him the same look she'd given him last night right before she told him to leave her alone.

Nicky backed off, not wanting to upset her again.

"I ate some leaves before I came outside," she explained, her voice softening.

Nicky motioned toward the bottle. "We need to get some of this into Scruggs. Don't you think it would help his strength?"

"We can't. It's dangerous to feed someone who's unconscious. He could choke. He should probably be on an intravenous unit, and that's way beyond our resources."

108

Marta winced as Nicky's comb caught a hidden tangle. She turned so she could see his face. "Speaking of Sid, may I ask you a question?"

Nicky knew what was coming.

"Why are you so nasty to him? I don't see him treating you badly. Ever since he showed up, you've acted as though you want to strangle him. If we hadn't rescued him, he'd probably be dead by now. Don't you realize that we saved his life?"

Nicky nodded, trying to think how he could get her off the subject of his eternal conflict with Scruggs.

"Besides," she continued, "if he hadn't been there when the bear came along, it'd be *you* lying unconscious in the lean-to instead of him."

The pleasure of touching Marta's hair disappeared as all the animosity he'd felt toward Scruggs the past three years sifted down on his shoulders with the thickening snowflakes. He shoved the comb back into his pocket, feeling weak again, overwhelmed by how much energy it took to hate someone.

"Yeah, there are reasons I've been acting the way I have toward Scruggs." He rested his head in his hands. Marta put her arm around his shoulders. Her touch comforted him.

Nicky turned his head to look at her. "It's too long a story to tell you right now. I don't think I have the strength." He gave her a sheepish look at his feeble explanation. But he was still trying to sort out the negative feelings he harbored for someone he didn't even know. Whose fault was it? His or Scruggs'?

"Yesterday," he continued, "I wanted to warn you about Scruggs, but my feelings for him have changed a lot in the last twenty-four hours. We'll talk after I get it all figured out. I promise." He liked making

109

promises for the future. It meant he was going to get out of here alive and *have* a future.

The look in her eyes was curious but understanding.

"Do you think Scruggs is dying?" Nicky blurted, not meaning to be so blunt. Sure, he disliked the guy, but not enough to wish him dead.

Marta withdrew her arm and began to shake. Alarmed, Nicky caught hold of her shoulders. "I'm sorry. I didn't mean to upset you."

"He may be dying, Nicky, but I don't know what else to do for him. I feel so *responsible*. I don't want another person's life to depend on me."

Nicky held on to her, not knowing what to say. Having Marta all to himself again was nice, but not at the expense of Scruggs' health. He'd make a point to subdue his good spirits.

"I keep wishing my grandfather would mentally send me instructions about what to do. He would know, but he's . . ."

"Whatever world your grandfather is in right now, I'm sure he's as proud of you as he ever was."

Marta looked as if she wanted to believe him.

"You haven't lost anybody yet, but you *have* managed to save three lives. You're batting a thousand right now, you know."

"I hadn't looked at it that way."

"It's a mind game a redheaded friend of mine taught me." He'd started to say *girl*friend, but changed it at the last second.

She actually laughed for the first time all morning. "You're feeding me my own medicine."

"Yeah, it's awful, isn't it?" He winked at her. "What you've done for Scruggs is more than the average person—including me—would know to do. I

110

didn't think about him going into shock, much less what signs to look for. I *know* you did the right thing."

Marta finally stopped shaking. "Maybe *you* were right, though. About carrying him out of here. Maybe we should try it right now—"

"No." Nicky shook his head as he thought it over. "Didn't you tell me the first rule of survival is to stay put and let yourself be found?"

"Stop quoting me." She tried to hide a smile.

"I am beginning to sound like you, aren't I? What a scary thought. Two encyclopedias, walking hand in hand through life." He pretended to shudder.

Marta ignored his teasing. "I wouldn't be as concerned if Scruggs were getting better, but his pulse is weaker this morning." Her voice trailed off at the end.

She began to draw pictures in the snow with her gloved fingers. "I want you to listen to me carefully," she began, not looking at him. "No matter what happens, Nicky, keep eating as much as possible to keep up your strength. And make sure Scruggs stays as warm, dry, and still as possible." She glanced at him. "Promise?"

Her words made him feel uneasy. Like an omen. A premonition. A curse. He attempted a laugh. "You sound as if you're going somewhere, Ms. Prigmore."

She held his gaze without answering.

"Marta, what's wrong?"

"Just promise you'll remember everything I've told you."

Chapter 17

As the day dragged on, the storm picked up in intensity. Nicky helped Marta secure more pine boughs on top of the lean-to to keep snow and icy gusts of wind from penetrating their fortress. Nicky now thought it was as dark as a tomb inside, then wished such a notion hadn't entered his mind.

They tried to erect another umbrella over the fire, but the snow was blowing sideways, making the flames sputter and die as soon as they ignited. Marta seemed unduly agitated about the matches they were wasting, so she made Nicky stop trying.

She was puzzling him. One minute she seemed all right, then the next minute she'd say something that didn't make any sense. Finally she stopped talking altogether.

He snacked on sap and leaves, the latter of which were getting harder to find. Most of them had turned brown or had fallen off their branches from the weight of this new snow. It took a lot of leaves to create a feeling of fullness, but after a while, he began to feel somewhat normal again. The sap was mostly sugar, so it gave him a boost of energy. And whenever he started feeling chilled enough to start shivering, he stepped outside to jog in place until he was semi-warm once more.

Nicky was almost comfortable for the first time since they'd been lost, but wished he had something to do, like develop pictures in the lean-to which—with the makeshift door attached—was as black inside as a photographer's darkroom.

Marta ate leaves and drank the water they'd melted in the lid of the bottle, but she refused to eat the sap, no matter how hard Nicky tried to persuade her. She seemed wobbly on her feet, and he thought the sap would give her additional strength, but she had a mind of her own, he'd discovered long ago.

Snow gusted against the lean-to throughout the day. Marta and Nicky took turns brushing off their distress signals, just in case. Nicky thought it was a waste of time, since it wasn't exactly a good day to be flying over the mountains, but what else did they have to do with their time?

During the afternoon, he dozed, deciding once he got tired enough, he'd sleep, no matter how cold he was. Lying in the dark next to Scruggs, he mentally focused on transferring the renewed strength he was feeling into Scruggs' body. Funny, he thought, I'd just convinced myself Scruggs was nothing but a big-talking coward, then he has to go and do something incredibly noble—like saving my life.

Would I have done the same for him? Nicky flashed back to the first night they were lost when he rescued Scruggs from under the tree. I guess I did save him, he reminded himself, or rather Marta saved him and I helped. Maybe Scruggs and I can call the score even.

Marta had been rubbing Scruggs' legs and arms to warm him and to keep his circulation going. Nicky thought about doing it, then decided he'd leave that up to Dr. Prigmore. Instead, he rolled over and went to sleep.

113

The distant hum of an airplane broke into his dream. Shaking the grogginess from his head, he was on his feet in one leap, bursting out the door. Large snowflakes slapped his face, blinding him for a moment. "Marta!"

The plane sounded far away. Maybe it was a commercial airliner, not a rescue plane.

"Marta!" he called again, but there was no answer. The humming was so faint, he could hardly hear it now. Starting off in the direction of the flat rock, he hollered at her. "Did you hear a plane?" Then he added, "Why didn't you come in when it started snowing this hard?" He reached the rock, but she wasn't there.

Maybe she did come in and I didn't notice, he thought, whirling around and heading back. The plane was gone now, as were Nicky's hopes of ever seeing home again. This latest storm promised to be the worst. It would surely destroy the rest of the leaves and plunge the wind chill factor to new depths. This is it, he said to himself as he retraced his steps, dropped to his knees, and peered into the darkness. "Marta, are you in here?"

No answer.

Panic overtook his insides. She hadn't tried to walk out of here to save them, had she? Thinking of the distress signals, he ran as best he could through the newly developing drifts. Keeping the signals cleaned off would be impossible under blizzard conditions, but he knew Marta would insist on trying.

Snow created a white wall in front of his face, stinging his eyes, entering his nostrils with each breath. Holding one side of his jacket to shield his face, he moved in the general direction of the signals until he stumbled across one log. "Marta!" he kept calling.

He half-crawled along the logs, finding it easier than trying to break through fresh snow with his aching legs. The wind whipped the scarf he'd tied around his head, yanking it free, but he kept going.

Something dark caught his eye. He moved toward it on pure adrenaline. Marta was slumped over a rock. One of her gloves had fallen off and her fingers were turning blue.

Nicky fell to his knees beside her, pulling her onto his lap. "What happened?" He shook her, but she didn't respond. Tearing off his own gloves, he rubbed her hand until the bluish color turned pink. Then he rescued her glove and jammed her fingers into it with shaking hands.

Nicky carried Marta back to the lean-to, noticing how little she weighed. Carrying her was like carrying a bag of softball equipment. He maneuvered through the door and laid her close to Scruggs, wrapping the blanket around both of them.

Hoisting the door in place to block the wind, he turned on the flashlight. What should he do? What would Marta do if the tables were turned? She'd check for injuries. He removed the blanket. She didn't appear to be injured. Her clothes weren't torn anywhere. What was wrong? She seemed fine before he'd fallen asleep. A little moody, but fine. Maybe she passed out from lack of food, yet they'd both eaten more today than they had all weekend, so that didn't seem likely.

Nicky's breathing seemed to stop as he searched his mind, looking for an explanation. He knew Scruggs was unconscious from a head injury, so he brushed hair away from her face, looking for bruises or bumps, then felt the back of her head. Maybe she had fallen and hit her head on a rock or log, or maybe she'd just fainted from overexertion.

In television shows, the rescuer always loosens the victim's collar to make breathing easier, so Nicky pulled the scarf from around Marta's neck and gingerly unbuttoned the top button of her shirt. A chain tangled in his fingers, so he drew it out, turning it over in his hand. He caught his breath as he read the message:

"I am a diabetic."

Chapter 18

"Oh, my God." Nicky froze as the word *diabetic* screamed at him from the necklace. "Why didn't you tell me?" Taking Marta by the shoulders, he gave her a hard shake. Then he realized she hadn't fainted. She was probably in a coma. An insulin coma.

Anger as well as fear flooded his body. "You're the most frustrating, independent, maddening . . ." His voice faltered. ". . . beautiful person I've ever met." Had she tried to tell him? He thought back to their last conversations. Maybe she had, but he hadn't been perceptive enough to hear what she was trying to say. Besides, how could his knowing about it have helped? By not telling, she was protecting him. Again.

It dawned on Nicky that any rescue team would have to know about Marta's condition. Surely her parents had alerted the authorities to the urgency of rescuing their daughter.

Nicky lashed out at the dark walls of the lean-to. "Isn't anyone coming for us?" He kicked the door, bursting outside to yell at the melting sky. "What stupid kind of rescue mission is this? One lousy helicopter in three days?" He pivoted, slipping, shaking his fist at the constant whiteness above, below, and all around him. "Where are you? They're gonna die if you don't get here fast. I can't . . . I can't . . .''

Nicky covered his face with his hands, swallowing tears. A few escaped down his cheek. Their salt stung his skin, raw from the harsh weather. When he pulled his hands away, he could barely see them a few inches from his face. "How can they find us now?" Up close, the lean-to looked like a giant, snow-covered boulder between two trees, and five steps away, it couldn't be seen at all.

Defeat rolled over him like an avalanche. Inside his head, he heard Marta's warning, "Don't get any wetter than you have to." As if obeying her silent command, he stumbled back inside the lean-to for shelter, pulling the door back in place.

No matter how impossible every situation had seemed up until now, Marta had always known what to do. And if she didn't know, she logically worked through the problem in her mind until she came up with a plan.

It had been fun with Marta here—like a game of survival on video, jumping over obstacles and zapping problems that loomed in front of them. Nicky had even allowed himself to enjoy it a little because he knew, down deep, they would be rescued. It had to be only a matter of time before they would be home, safe, warm, and dry, laughing about their mistakes and bragging about their accomplishments. His mind refused to accept any other ending.

But his mind was questioning now. The game was over. How could Marta leave him to face this alone? He wasn't like her. He didn't have a plan.

Nicky lay next to her, wrapping his arms around her still form. "Marta, tell me what to do."

As soon as the words had formed, he remembered.

She *had* told him what to do. Of course. When they were sitting on the rock, Marta had seemed upset and far away. She knew something like this might happen. She'd said, "Promise me, no matter what happens, you'll continue to eat to maintain your strength, and you'll keep Scruggs as warm, dry, and still as possible."

She knew.

Nicky closed his eyes. What was it Marta's grandfather used to say? It's better to do something, even if it's wrong, than to do nothing at all?

"But," Nicky argued out loud, "this is different. This is a life or death decision. I don't want to be responsible for someone else's life." He suddenly remembered Marta saying those exact words about Scruggs.

He sat up. Okay. I'm going to do *something*. Marta would think the problem through first. Diabetes. What do I know about diabetes? Nothing. He remembered discussing it in Biology class, but, as usual, he hadn't paid much attention because the topic didn't interest him.

He mentally projected himself to his desk in Biology and tried to tune in on what the teacher was saying. It was a memory trick he'd read about once, useful during exams. But it'd been a year since he'd taken Biology, so it was hard. And his mind wasn't exactly sharp right now.

Nicky struggled to focus his thoughts. All he could remember was the textbook definition of diabetes: *A disease in which the body does not produce enough insulin to burn up sugar.* He'd had to memorize that for a test. Of course he knew diabetics had to take daily shots of insulin, and without them, the disease would be fatal. What more did he need to remember?

119

Without insulin, there was nothing he could do to save Marta. It was hopeless. A game he couldn't win.

Wait a minute. Maybe Marta had brought insulin with her. She'd brought everything else in the whole wide world, hadn't she? Nicky grabbed the battered backpack, dumping the contents under the glare of the flashlight, sorting through it quickly.

Nothing.

He thought for a moment, then searched the pockets of Marta's jacket. There it was—one vial of insulin, three-quarters empty, with a few disposable syringes.

Nicky was confused when he saw the insulin. If she hadn't run out, then that wasn't the problem. So why was she unconscious? She must have been rationing the insulin like they'd rationed the food, not knowing how long they'd be away from civilization.

There was nothing more to do except grudgingly prepare for another cold night in this prison. He never felt more alone in his entire life. As a final gesture of hope, he forced himself outside to brush snow off the distress signals one more time. But new snow covered them as quickly as he swept it off.

He thought about cleaning off the lean-to also, but he sensed that the layer of snow sealed their shelter, making it more heat efficient, which was good. He decided to leave the lean-to buried.

Buried.

He hated that word. It was the one thing that bothered him most about dying. Dying didn't seem as bad as being buried forever. Six feet underground. Nicky shuddered, remembering a book he'd read about a girl who was buried alive. Her casket had been opened later, revealing that she'd tried to claw her way out before she suffocated to death. Her nails were bloody, broken to the quick. Her face was twisted in the panic of inevitable death. He tried not to imagine the terror that had gripped the girl's mind before she died. He hoped he was good and dead before they buried him.

Dying out here in the wilderness meant his body would be at the mercy of wild animals and the elements. What if the person who discovered his remains was a kid from next year's Weekender? How gruesome. Nicky shuddered again. He could almost handle it for himself, but Marta deserved more. She was special. She deserved to live.

The feeling came over him as bluntly as if a tree had fallen and knocked him on the head. He cared about Marta, more than he wanted to admit. Was he falling in love with her? He didn't know; he'd never fallen in love before. But the way she made him feel, he never wanted to let go of that.

The emotions deepening inside of him for Marta were so strong, he found himself wishing he could trade places with her right now. He was willing to die if it meant she would live. The reality of his feelings hit him hard.

"I love you," he whispered into the darkness, just to hear how it sounded. He'd never said those words before.

"Please don't die."

He'd never said those words before either.

Chapter 19

It was eerie, sitting in total darkness, listening to the storm rage outside. A few gusts threatened to topple the lean-to. Nicky prayed it would hold. How could he protect Scruggs and Marta without a shelter?

Other than the storm, it was too quiet. He remembered Marta's method of singing to herself to make time pass, but he felt stupid, sitting in the dark, singing. And the only songs he could think of were mushy love songs which only made him feel worse.

Nicky was growing numb from cold. He had no feeling in his toes and it worried him. Maybe he should try another fire, closer to the lean-to, sheltering it from the wind with the door he'd made. It was worth a try. He worried the others might not survive without a fire's warmth.

Nicky turned on the flashlight to locate the film container which held the matches Marta had dipped in polish.

It was empty.

Fear tickled through him. Their matches were gone. Marta knew. That's why she discouraged him from trying to light another fire. And she chose not to tell, to keep him from getting alarmed. He glanced toward her, shaking his head. Her time for protecting him was over. Now he had to protect her—and himself.

Nicky replaced the door, hugging himself to get warm. He'd searched Marta's pockets earlier; maybe he should sort through Scruggs' pockets, too. He vaguely remembered seeing Scruggs smoke. Maybe he had matches.

Nicky climbed over Marta, who now occupied the middle, and searched Scruggs' pockets. He found a cigarette lighter. "Thanks," he whispered, feeling a glimmer of hope trickle back into his mind. Returning to his original plan, Nicky stripped dry bark from the underside of the lean-to to use as kindling.

Angling the door to block the blowing snow, he anchored it to the lean-to with his own shoelaces, bracing the backpack against the other side. Nicky's hands shook as he cleared the fire circle of snow. He wanted to hurry and light the kindling before it got wet.

He coughed as smoke filled his lungs. Backing away, he cheered the small fire on until it took. Finally the few skimpy flames grew larger and lit up the night.

Forcing down the last of the leaves and sap, Nicky enjoyed the forgotten sensation of fullness. He filled the plastic bottle with snow so he'd have water to drink in the morning. Tomorrow he'd collect more sap, unless it had stopped flowing.

Now he understood why Marta had been reluctant to eat the sap. A diabetic eating pure sugar with limited insulin was committing slow suicide.

Nicky checked on the others, making sure they were well covered with the blanket. He wished the fire would fill their shelter with as much warmth as it was smoke. Coughing, he lay down as close to Marta as he could without jostling her, but he couldn't sleep. The day's events rolled through his brain like a horror movie.

123

He knew it was Scruggs' last night. Without medical attention, his wounds were probably getting infected. Scruggs' breathing was barely audible now, but more than that, he'd gone a day and a half without food or water. Marta had been right about Scruggs' pulse getting weaker, too. Nicky tried not to think any further than that. He'd never seen a dead person before, much less someone he knew. He'd worry about what to do when it actually happened.

Ashes to ashes, dust to dust singsonged through his mind.

And Marta. Nicky wished he knew more about her illness. Why hadn't she talked to him about it? He didn't know how long she could survive without insulin. Should he give her what was left in the vial? The uncertainty haunted him. Would he be saving her life or speeding up her death? He hated himself for not knowing. A lump rose in his throat as he shifted closer to her. It wasn't fair.

Nicky remembered the word game he used to play in elementary school, counting the number of letters in a girl's name. Nicky and Marta. Five letters each. Marta was bound to be his forever girlfriend. Ha. Why was it every girl he developed a crush on had the same number of letters in her name as he had? Maybe he should call her Martinella to break the spell.

Rolling onto his back, Nicky dozed, but nightmares crept into the corners of his mind like shadows of monsters. Memories of an article he'd read on how the body of a starving person begins to digest its own insides made his eyes bolt open to consciousness.

He had to get out of here to save the others. There was no question about it. As soon as it was light, he would walk out. He'd just keep walking until he found a road, a house, a person—something. Of course, if he headed in the wrong direction, he'd walk deeper and deeper into the national forest, which stretched on into endless wilderness. He assumed that's what the three of them had done already—hiked in the wrong direction. Still, he could not sit here and watch his companions die. He had to try. Or die trying.

Nicky felt better as the idea cemented in his mind. Now he had a plan, just like Marta. He'd be able to move a lot faster alone than the three of them together. Why hadn't he started off today? He was crazy not to. Why did he keep expecting the best, without preparing for the worst? Well, tomorrow he would take fate by storm. He'd leave everything behind—the lighter, a fresh pile of leaves and some sap, in case Marta or Scruggs woke up. If luck was with him, he'd be back with help before nightfall.

Nicky fell into an uneasy sleep. He dreamed he and Luker were swimming in Lake Chautauqua. Suddenly Luker was drowning. Nicky swam as fast as his arms could pull him through the water, but could never get close enough to save his friend. Luker kept calling for him as he went under again and again and again.

"Luker!" Nicky jolted awake. His heart was pounding. Lying still, waiting for his breathing to return to normal, he remembered how alone he was, out in the middle of nowhere, totally at nature's mercy. He wished daylight would hurry so he could be on his way. He also wished he hadn't read so many science fiction books lately about strange happenings in the forest in the middle of the night. He longed to escape into a deep sleep. Smoke tickled his nose as he realized that's all that was left of his fire, but he was too exhausted to get up and pull the door closed.

Do people's lives really flash before their eyes as they die? he wondered. His own life seemed so uneventful, not to mention short. Uneventful until now, he reminded himself. He always assumed he would live forever—one reason he hadn't made any decisions about his future after high school. The career counselor at Mitchell High acted as if Nicky's whole life had to be planned before he graduated.

But Nicky hadn't decided what he wanted to do with his life. Track would always be a hobby, but not a career. It was more likely he'd turn his love for photography into a career. Why was the school counselor rushing him? He was only fifteen. He still had a few more years to think about it.

It made him feel uneasy that his future was so hazy. He wondered if having definite plans would let fate know he intended to live a long, full life. The gray cloud of his future seemed an open invitation to destiny that death wouldn't cancel any terrific plans he might have made. The thought made him shiver.

Marta had planned her future, of course. She'd told him she wanted to major in Botany and become a forest ranger. Nicky hoped with all his heart she got a chance to live out her dream.

Once again, he slept.

Sometime in the middle of the night, Nicky became aware of the presence of an animal outside the lean-to. He had sensed it, probably as it had sensed him. Forcing his mind awake, he rolled to his hands and knees. His heart was beating like crazy, and he could scarcely breathe. The dead fire was still smoking. Quickly he knocked away the backpack and yanked the door shut, scattering the hot ashes. Even though the door was flimsy, he felt safer with it shut.

Whatever it was came around to the front. He could hear it sniffing at the door. Nicky wondered if shouting would scare the animal away or make it attack. He blocked the image of a bear out of his mind. If they'd run out of leaves to eat, then so had the bears. But wouldn't the first heavy snow of the year have sent the animals into hibernation?

If not, he was trapped. A captive meal.

Was there a tree outside he could make a dash for if he got the chance? Nicky scrapped the impulse. He couldn't leave Marta to the mercy of a wild animal—or Scruggs either, his conscience told him. Damn this animal. He wouldn't let it ruin his plans for tomorrow.

He remembered the first encounter with the bear, and how Marta had warned him to stay still so the animal would leave them alone. And it did. Maybe he should lie down and play dead.

He tried it, but he couldn't lie still. He was so scared, his entire body shook. His teeth were even chattering. Thoughts jumbled his mind: the new aware- ness of his love for Marta, his animosity for Scruggs— complicated by his concern for Scruggs' life—and his own fear. He was absolutely terrified for his life.

Tears came into his eyes. He bit his lip until it bled. *After all I've been through, I'm not going to lie here and cry. I'm not going to give up and do nothing.*

The animal scratched at the door, trying to stick its nose through. As the door broke loose and flipped to one side, the dark form of the animal loomed in the doorway.

Nicky froze, anticipating the animal's movements. It was too dark to determine the hunkered outline, telling him what it was. The animal entered the lean-to, heading straight toward Marta.

"That's it," Nicky muttered with a clenched jaw. Rising abruptly, he lunged at the animal, startling it, knocking it through the doorway, rolling in the snow

127

on top of the clawing, biting form, then rolling again until the growling animal was on top of him, tearing at his jacket with its teeth.

It was a dog.

Nicky had heard stories of wild dogs running in packs in the mountains. They would attack and kill a bear for food.

Wrestling the animal, Nicky tried to gain his footing in the slippery snow so he could reach for a log from the fire and bash the animal's head. Suddenly there was another dog at his back. Whipping about, he was instantly blinded by a flashlight. Someone shouted and the dogs backed off. Frightened, Nicky shielded his eyes to make out the face of a tall, bearded man. The man's clothes and beard were frosted with ice.

"Who are you?" Nicky sputtered, coming to his feet.

"Calm down, son," the man retorted in a gruff voice. He bent to reassure the prancing animals before he spoke again. "Is your name Brooks?" he asked.

Nicky stared at the man, his mind unable to register what was happening.

"We all smelled smoke," the man continued, softening his voice, "so we headed in this direction, wondering how on earth a fire could get started in the middle of this damn blizzard."

Nicky became aware of other voices and lights in the forest. He reached to tilt the blinding light out of his eyes, catching sight of the emblem on the man's jacket: Colorado Mountain Search and Rescue Team.

Chapter 20

Nicky didn't like being in Denver General Hospital, especially since he was the healthiest one of the three. But the doctors insisted on observing him for a few days since he'd suffered mild frostbite, and, embarrassingly enough, a few dog bites. He did prefer his window view of the snow-capped mountains from a distance, as opposed to being stranded in the middle of them.

It surprised him that the search team was operating late at night in a blizzard, but a few hardy volunteers had persisted, knowing how dangerous Marta's condition was and how little time they had left to find her. Nicky was thankful for their dedication, risking their own lives to search for the missing group. Of course, the team hadn't known Scruggs was with them, but were relieved to find all three at once.

Nicky had spent the rest of the night watching a paramedic hover over Marta. Her coma was the result of too much insulin instead of not enough, as he had guessed. Marta had been diagnosed with juvenile diabetes several weeks earlier and had been warned again and again to take her insulin regularly. Her mistake had been in not adjusting the dose of insulin to the lesser amount of food she'd been eating, as well as to her increased physical activity.

It surprised Nicky that the rescue team waited until morning to airlift them out of the mountains. But it was easier to treat Marta and Scruggs right where they were. At least there were lots of warm blankets and a thermos of hot barley soup for Nicky, as well as compliments for his clever idea of building a smoke signal to attract the rescuers.

Nicky just smiled. He'd attracted the rescuers. He'd saved all three of them. By himself. By accident.

Hospitals were more boring than being lost in the mountains, even though Erin had just called to fill him in on the rest of the Weekender he'd managed to miss.

The softball tournament had been called off due to the unexpected snowstorm, and the scavenger hunt had been won by two girls Nicky didn't even know.

The disappearance of the three of them had cast a gloomy atmosphere over the rest of the Weekender, according to Erin. Especially after Shana led a group to rescue Scruggs and he was nowhere to be found. She also said Shana had shown up at the Saturday night dance wearing some senior's ring. So much for Shana, Nicky thought.

The only other news was that Mr. German and Ms. Egan had planned on announcing their engagement during the Weekender, but had been so upset over losing three of their charges, they'd postponed the big announcement until after everyone was home safe.

Nicky was tired of doing nothing. Putting on his robe, he started down the hallway to visit Marta. Rounding a corner, he bumped into Luker, coming to see him with a stack of school books and a backpack.

"How ya doing, buddy?" Luker asked, grinning at him.

"I've been better, thanks. You wouldn't consider smuggling in a pepperoni pizza for me, would you?"

Luker's eyes scanned the hall as he lowered his voice. "What do you think's in the backpack?"

As they got to Marta's room, she was leaving, carrying a gift in her hand. She looked terrific in a nutmeg-brown bathrobe that matched her eyes. Color had returned to her face, even though her cheekbones still looked prominent. Her broken glasses had been replaced with new ones. This time, with burgundy frames. To Nicky, she looked gorgeous.

"Hi guys," she said. "Come with me. My mom dropped this off for me to give to Sid. He's allowed to have visitors now."

"Sid?" Luker repeated.

"Scruggs," Nicky explained, watching his friend's face. "It's a long story." His stomach knotted, wondering why Marta was giving a present to Scruggs instead of him. Jealousy, his mind warned.

Marta gave him a sidelong glance as if she were reading his thoughts. "Nicky, he's going to be in the hospital a lot longer than you are. He may even lose a few toes from frostbite." She took his hand as they walked.

Luker hung back. "Listen, you two go on. I'll dump these in your room, Nick," he said, holding up the books and the hidden pizza. "Then I gotta leave."

Nicky grabbed his friend's arm, stopping him. "Come on, Luker, it's okay. Up there," he gestured out a window toward the mountains, "I found out that way down deep, Scruggs is actually human." Nicky didn't know any other way to put it. He knew he and Scruggs would never become friends, but from now on they'd see each other through different eyes. As equals. And he knew, without bringing it up, Scruggs would never call him Nicholas again.

Luker wasn't easily convinced.

131

"Scruggs has been through a lot—believe me."

"Yeah, I guess you're right," Luker admitted. "At school he's become something of a hero. They call him the guy who survived a broken leg, hypothermia, and a bear attack."

"Not to mention spending three nights with Martinella Lee Prigmore," Nicky added as Marta punched him playfully in the jaw. He caught her hand which held the gift. "What is this, anyway?"

"It's a book called *Tips on Backpacking and How to Survive*."

Luker laughed. "Did you write it, Marta?"

"No, but I starred in the movie with Nicky Brooks."

They groaned as she linked her arms through theirs and led them down the hall to visit Scruggs.

Author's Note

The Colorado Rescue Board estimates that there are 500 to 700 annual back country mishaps which require efforts by nonprofit search and rescue organizations or sheriffs' departments. These include hikers or campers getting lost, stranded, or needing emergency medical attention. The rate is higher in the wilderness areas because of greater risk factors and remoteness from roads.

Black bear sightings are common (although not counted) in most of Colorado's mountains. Several areas of the state claim a higher population of bears; therefore sightings in those areas are more frequent.

Information provided by
the United States Forest Service,
Rocky Mountain Region

DIAN CURTIS REGAN grew up near the Colorado Rockies and spent many summers backpacking and camping. Camp Chautauqua is based on the Trojan Ranch on Gold Hill in Boulder Canyon, where many Colorado students attend various versions of the Weekender.

Dian is a board member for the National Association for Young Writers and a Regional Advisor for the Society of Children's Book Writers. She presently lives in Oklahoma City, where she serves as an artist-in-residence for the state.

Avon Flare Mysteries
by Edgar Award-Winning Author

JAY BENNETT

THE DEATH TICKET 89597-8/$2.50 US/$3.25 Can

Trouble arrives when a lottery ticket turns up a winner—worth over six million dollars—and maybe more than one life!

THE EXECUTIONER 79160-9/$2.50 US/2.95 Can

Indirectly responsible for a friend's death, Bruce is consumed by guilt—until someone is out to get *him*.

And Spine-tingling Suspense
from the author of *Slumber Party*

CHRISTOPHER PIKE

CHAIN LETTER 89968-X/$2.50 US/$3.50 Can

One by one, the chain letter was coming to each of them ...demanding dangerous, impossible deeds. None in the group wanted to believe it—until the accidents—and the dying—started happening!

ATTENTION TEENAGE WRITERS!
You can win a $2,500 book contract and have your novel published as the winner of the 1989 Avon Flare Young Adult Novel Competition!

Here are the submission requirements:

We will accept completed manuscripts from authors between the ages of thirteen and eighteen from January 1, 1989 through August 31, 1989 at the following address:

The Editors, Avon Flare Novel Competition
Avon Books, Room 818, 105 Madison Avenue
New York, New York 10016

Each manuscript should be approximately 125 to 200 pages, or about 30,000 to 50,000 words (based on 250 words per page).

All manuscripts must be typed, double-spaced, on a single side of the page only.

Along with your manuscript, please enclose a letter that includes a short description of your novel, your name, address, telephone number, and your age.

You are eligible to submit a manuscript if you will be no younger than thirteen and no older than eighteen years of age as of December 31, 1988. Enclose <u>a self-addressed, stamped envelope</u> for the return of your manuscript, and a <u>self-addressed stamped postcard</u> so that we can let you know we have received your submission.

PLEASE BE SURE TO RETAIN A COPY OF YOUR MANUSCRIPT. WE CANNOT BE RESPONSIBLE FOR MANUSCRIPTS.

The Prize: If you win this competition your novel will be published by Avon Flare for an advance of $2,500.00 against royalties. A parent or guardian's signature (consent) will be required on your publishing contract.

We reserve the right to use the winning author's name and photograph for advertising, promotion, and publicity.

If you wish to be notified of the winner, please enclose a self-addressed, stamped postcard for this purpose. Notification will also be made to major media.

<u>Waiting Time:</u> We will try to review your manuscript within three months. However, it is possible that we will hold your manuscript for as long as a year, or until the winner is announced.

VOID WHERE PROHIBITED BY LAW.